CRUEL DADDY

BOSTON MAFIA DONS

BIANCA COLE

CONTENTS

1. Aida — 1
2. Milo — 9
3. Aida — 19
4. Milo — 27
5. Aida — 39
6. Milo — 53
7. Aida — 65
8. Milo — 73
9. Aida — 81
10. Milo — 91
11. Aida — 99
12. Milo — 107
13. Aida — 115
14. Milo — 127
15. Aida — 141
16. Milo — 151
17. Aida — 161
18. Milo — 171
19. Aida — 183
20. Milo — 191
21. Aida — 203
22. Milo — 217
23. Aida — 227
24. Milo — 237
25. Aida — 247
26. Milo — 255
27. Aida — 265

28. Milo 275
Epilogue 289

Also by Bianca Cole 303
About the Author 307

Cruel Daddy Copyright © 2022 Bianca Cole

All Rights Reserved.
No part of this publication may be reproduced, stored, or transmitted in any form or by any means, electronic, mechanical, photocopying, recording, scanning, or otherwise without written permission from the publisher. It is illegal to copy this book, post it to a website, or distribute it by any other means without permission.

This novel is entirely a work of fiction. The names, characters and incidents portrayed in it are the work of the author's imagination. Any resemblance to actual persons, living or dead, events or localities is entirely coincidental.

Warning: the unauthorized reproduction or distribution of this copyrighted work is illegal. Criminal copyright infringement, including infringement without monetary gain, is investigated by the FBI and is punishable by up to 5 years in prison and a fine of $250,000.

Book cover design by Deliciously Dark Designs

Editing by: Rainlyt Editing

BLURB

Cruelty is his middle name, and I'm at his mercy.

My father has kept me locked away in an ivory tower. I thought he wanted to protect me, but he only wanted to protect his asset. An untouched, sheltered mob princess is worth a lot of money to the right buyer.

My father's greed means Sicily is no longer big enough for him. I'm shipped across the Atlantic to Boston to marry a man I've never met, whose reputation for cruelty reaches as far as the shores of Sicily.

Milo Mazzeo is as dark as they come. He's a ruthless don with no morals, and he's about to become my husband. It's clear from the moment we meet that we have nothing in common.

Once we say I do, he tells me that I'm his possession. I must do whatever he says. I'm nothing more than a slave to tend to his every whim and need. If he thinks I'm going to accept my fate without a fight, he is mistaken.

I always expected to marry for love, but all I feel is hate toward this beautiful beast. They say there is a fine line between love and hate. Could the fire of hatred really twist into something more?

*Trigger Warning: This book contains scenes some

may find upsetting, including dub-con and BDSM. If this kind of material offends you, then this may be one to skip.

1

AIDA

The blistering heat of the sun radiates over my skin as I walk to the top of the cliff. Today has been a beautiful summer's day. I spent it on the beach with Gia, one of my best friends.

It was a shame that I couldn't stay for the sunset. My father insisted I meet him atop the cliff we used to come to when my mother was alive. We used to spend blissful days on this cliff having family picnics.

My bodyguard, Aldo, follows close behind me. He's a permanent shadow I can't shake. Once I reach the top, I notice my father standing at the cliff edge. He is staring out over the glimmering, azure Sicilian Sea. It's such a beautiful view. Few people are lucky enough to call such a stunning island home. It's a blessing, even if my father keeps me so frequently locked in our home. He tells me it's too dangerous for me to wander the beaches alone. No matter how much I long to find some peace and solitude, Aldo is always with me.

Oddly, my father has asked me to meet him atop this cliff today. We haven't been up here together since I was a little girl. Back then, my mother was alive, and I would say we were a happy family despite the horrors my father dealt with daily. It's crazy how time changes everything.

I look at my father properly, studying the way his shoulders sag under the weight of the empire he's holding up. It's been ten years since my mother's murder, and since then, he has become distant. Before her death, our family was close.

I was only eleven years old when she was murdered by one of my father's enemies. It was hard to come to terms with at such a young age, but harder still when my father practically disappeared from my life for a year in a crazy vendetta to seek revenge. Time has healed the wounds, but I struggle to accept the reason for her death to this day. She was collateral damage in a power struggle between my father and another Italian family.

He turns to gaze at me but doesn't smile. I remember his smile from when I was little, but I haven't seen it since. "Aida, please join me," he says, holding out his hand to me.

I do as he says, taking his hand and joining him near the edge of the white, rocky cliffs. "How are you, Father?"

He swallows hard, his Adam's apple bobbing as he does. "As well as I can be. As always, work is stressful."

I nod in response. My father rarely talks to me about his work, which I know isn't legal. No matter how much my father believes he has successfully sheltered me from the truth, he's wrong. I know he runs the Sicilian mafia, and his father before him did the same—our family has held power on these shores for generations.

He glances at me and squeezes my hand. "I asked you to meet me here as I have some news, Amore."

I smile at him, meeting his gaze. "What is it?"

He looks uncertain before speaking. "I've found you a husband."

My eyes widen. "What?" I stare at him in shock, as he's never warned me about any intention to marry me off. I only turned twenty-one two months ago.

He smiles and takes my other hand to pull me to face him. "I've kept you safe, Aida, but now it's time another man takes the role of your protector." His jaw clenches slightly. "Milo Mazzeo wants to marry you in his hometown, Boston."

Milo Mazzeo.

It feels like my world spins the moment he says his name. I drop my father's hands and step away from him. I've never met the man he speaks of. Still, everyone knows his name—he's infamous even here in Sicily for his brutality and cruelty, particularly with anyone who disrespects him.

Why would my father ship me over to a man like him?

I shake my head. "No, I won't marry that man. He's as evil as they get, Father." I feel sick to my stomach at the suggestion. "I don't need a protector. I want to marry a man I love, not by an arrangement."

My father's smile drops, and his eyes narrow. "You'll do as you are told, Aida."

The thought of living in the same city as Milo Mazzeo, let alone as his wife, scares me. The horror stories I've heard about the way he treats people are almost impossible to believe. He's as cruel as they come.

"Why would you give me to a man like him?" I ask, emotion clawing at my throat.

My father's jaw clenches. "It was always my intention to marry you to a man who can increase the power of our family's business, Aida." He grabs my shoulders. "I don't want any disobedience. You will marry Milo Mazzeo, end of discussion."

I stare in shock at my father, wondering if this is the reason why he's been so protective of me since my mother was murdered. "I thought you cared about me."

He won't meet my gaze, staring out over the sea instead. "Your mother's death changed me, Aida. I hate how much you remind me of her. If you're in Boston, that will solve the problem." He glares at me with a coldness that cuts through me deeply. "I don't want you here."

Tears prickle at my eyes. All I've ever done is adore my father. It's difficult to process the words he's saying to me as he rips my heart from my chest. I've always known he's a dark and haunted man—he'd have to be to do the things he does--but he always treated me well.

"What would mother think if she could see what you are doing to her only child?" I ask, feeling the emotion and anger rise inside of me.

My father's eyes flash with rage. "Don't fucking talk about her." He grabs my wrist forcefully. "She can't see because she is dead and gone, Aida." He shakes his head frantically. "There's no such thing as happy endings in our world, so you will have to accept your fate with dignity."

I fight and rip my wrist from his grasp, rushing away from him. It's hard to believe that this is how my father feels about me. All these years, his intention to sell me off motivated his overprotective nature. I walk away from the cliff edge, needing some space to process what he told me.

Boston can't be like Sicily—nowhere is. I hate the idea of leaving the place I've called home all my life. Tears trickle down my face as I stare across the sea, wishing my mother was still alive. If she were, none of this would be happening.

Life won't be worth living if I'm a possession of that beast. A man who has done and does unspeakable things, even for the head of a mafia family. As I stare over the cliff, I wonder if it would be easier to take my own life.

I think you must have a certain mindset to do so,

and although my future looks bleak, I wouldn't be able to do it. The beauty of the world will still surround me, and I must be strong. My mother always taught me to be strong and face my fears with my head held high.

I must do what she always taught me when I face my husband-to-be. Milo Mazzeo is twisted and sick, but I won't let it faze me.

"Aida, come away from there," my father says with concern—concern only for his deal falling through if I were to die. The anger in his voice has diminished, but I know when I turn around, he will look at me with a hatred I never realized existed.

It feels like I'm in a nightmare, as I never expected my father to do something so heartless. Perhaps I've been blind to the truth about him. He's been broken since my mother's murder, and the more time that passes, the more twisted he becomes.

I turn to face him, wiping the tears from my cheeks. "When will I be leaving?"

He glances behind me at Aldo and gives him a nod. "Right away."

Aldo comes forward and grabs hold of my shoulders. "The car is waiting to take you to the airport. All your things are packed and on the plane."

I stare at my father, dumbfounded by the sudden rush to ship me away. "Won't you at least let me say goodbye to my friends?"

My father shakes his head. "I won't risk you running. Aldo is to take you straight to the airport."

It feels like my entire world is being torn apart as I struggle to draw breath into my lungs. I accept that my father has the power to rip me away from my home and force me into Milo Mazzeo's arms, but cruelly forcing it on me so suddenly with no chance to say goodbye to my friends and my home is unfair.

I step forward, breaking away from Aldo's grasp. The coldness of my father's stare makes me sure I can't reason with him. I run for the way back down off the cliff, despite knowing I'll probably be caught.

I'm only a few feet from the descent when Aldo's arms wrap around my waist. He drags me back to my father while I fight in his grasp.

"Stop this at once, Aida." My father grabs my wrists hard and forces me to stop fighting.

He nods at Aldo, and before I register his plan, a needle stabs into my neck.

"What the hell?" I ask, stumbling to grab the place on my neck where they drugged me.

"It is best if you can't fight. By the time you wake up, you will be in America," my father says with no sign of remorse.

I shake my head in utter disbelief. "You drugged me?" My vision blurs as I stumble into Aldo. He holds onto me, taking my weight. The warmth of the sun penetrates my skin as my head spins.

"It's for your own good," my father says, making my chest ache.

None of this is for my own good. My father's greed

is more important than his only child. Pain clutches around my throat as I try not to cry—crying right now would be pathetic.

"You will be in Boston and married before you know it. Your life here will be a memory. Embrace it," my father says, staring into my eyes with such coldness. "Goodbye." He turns away and walks toward the edge of the cliff as my vision darkens.

"Aldo, please don't do this," I plead.

He wraps his arms around my waist and hoists me over his shoulder. "I'm sorry. I don't have a choice."

It feels like the world spins as the drugs infect my bloodstream. I don't have long until I'll be unconscious and ripped away from everything I've known and loved. My father is about to thrust me into the hands of a man so cruel I can't even fathom what he might do to me.

The last thing I remember is the warmth of the Sicilian sun penetrating my skin and the far-off sound of waves crashing against the shore as everything goes dark.

2

MILO

I check my tie in the mirror, making sure I look presentable. Image is key wherever I go. Although I don't really care what my wife-to-be thinks of me, I won't make a bad first impression.

Fabio Alteri controls Sicily and has a perfect position in the Mediterranean. I know how important binding our two organizations is if I wish to grow beyond North America's walls. It's the only reason I agreed to marry his daughter.

Ambition has always been a strength of mine and it knows no bounds. My father was lazy and content being average. Global expansion has been on my list of goals ever since he died. Fabio approaching me sped up those plans, giving me that chance, and I would not let it pass me by. I met him in Sicily two months ago to agree on the deal, which involved me marrying his daughter. A woman I've never met.

I never wanted to marry, but I agree that it's the only way to secure our partnership since Aida Alteri is his only heir. We met two months ago to agree to the wedding date and finalize the contract and he waited until four days before the wedding to send her to me. The man is ruthless, since he isn't even accompanying her or attending the wedding.

Aida is twenty-one years old, and according to her father, she's a virgin. A wife wasn't in my life plans, but I'll enjoy breaking in a virgin. She'll be nothing more than my slave and possession. Her father must not care for her much, sending her across the Atlantic alone into my hands.

I check my watch. Her plane is due to touch down within an hour. I turn away from the mirror and glance around the office, making sure I have everything I need. Once satisfied, I walk out of the room.

My capo, Piero, is waiting outside of my office. He averts his gaze as I approach as a sign of respect, keeping his head bowed.

"Sir, I have news on Luigi."

Luigi is one of my soldiers who screwed up a drug deal yesterday evening and hasn't been seen since. "You found him?"

Piero nods, meeting my gaze. "Yes, we have him locked in the basement." He tilts his head to the side. "What do you want me to do with him?"

I clench my jaw, knowing I don't have the time to torture him thoroughly myself right now. My future wife is already impeding my day-to-day life and I don't like it. "Start torturing him for information. I want to know what happened, but make sure he's alive when I get back." I meet Piero's gaze. "You know his life is mine to take."

Piero nods. "Of course, sir." He glances at the door to my office. "Do you need me to make any arrangements for your wedding or wife to be?"

I raise a brow. "No, all is in hand. I am going to meet her at the airport in—" I check my watch, "forty minutes, so I need to get going. James is waiting with the car outside."

Piero bows his head. "I'm sorry for keeping you, sir."

I shake my head. "Don't worry about it." I walk away down the corridor. "Remember, Luigi is mine," I remind him as I walk toward the exit of my home.

The drive to the airport is about forty minutes, which means I might be late. My fiancé will have to learn that she waits as long as necessary for me. Fabio has promised me she will be easy to deal with. I can't handle a stuck-up mafia princess who gives me grief, but if she is a brat, I'll soon beat it out of her. I don't need any trouble from a woman. All I need is a submissive that will do as she is told and be mine to fuck when I want. I won't tolerate disobedience, and if she's heard any rumors about me, she'll know not to push me.

A dark and twisted part of me hopes she does not know what kind of man I am. I want a sheltered and innocent woman to take and mold. Fabio assured me that his daughter is beautiful. Beauty is subjective, and all fathers believe their daughters are beautiful.

Olivia approaches me, carrying my briefcase. "James is ready for you, sir, and I got together the papers you wanted to go through in the car." She passes me the case.

I nod, taking the briefcase. "Thank you. Please ensure that the household staff has the room next to mine prepared for my future wife."

Olivia bows her head. "It's already in hand, sir."

I nod. "Good." I walk toward the limousine in front of my home. James is standing next to it with the door held open for me. I always expect the best from my staff.

"Good morning, sir," James says.

Is it a good morning, though?

I grit my teeth. "Morning," I reply.

The fact that I've got to miss out on the torturing of a man who has screwed us over and leave it to my capo has gotten under my skin. I live to rule by an iron fist, and meeting my future wife is getting in the way of that. I hate being inconvenienced, and it's Fabio's fault for not accompanying his daughter, leaving me to meet her.

I slide into the back of my limo and sit forward with my hands clasped together. A sense of foreboding sweeps over me. I'm never uncertain about anything I do in life, but marrying Fabio Alteri's daughter gives me second thoughts, and I haven't even met her yet.

Marriage is a necessity. My father believed that, but I don't. If I want a successor, I can fuck any whore who is happy to carry my baby for a shitload of money. There's nothing people won't do if you pay well. I know that my empire needs a successor, but being a father is not something that appeals to me.

Maybe marrying Alteri's daughter is an ideal situation. I can play with her until I get bored, get her pregnant, and then she can look after my heir. There's no time in my life for a woman or a child.

The journey feels like it drags as I read my emails, noticing one from Fabio. His daughter wasn't all too pleased by the arrangement. The sick and twisted side of me rejoices at the news. I feel Aida is going to be a challenge. I never back down from a challenge and the news puts me at ease as we drive toward the private airstrip.

We arrive at the private airstrip before the plane has arrived. James parks next to the gate where the plane is due to pull up. A few minutes pass by before James's voice comes through the intercom. "The plane has landed, sir."

I clear my throat. "Very well, I'll wait outside." It's a warm summer's day, so I slip on my sunglasses. I wait for James to open the door to my limousine.

James opens the door and I slide out, just as the plane rolls past me and turns into the gate.

I walk to the front of the vehicle and lean on the hood, crossing my arms over my chest. My future wife is on that plan. I hate the way my stomach twists at the mere thought of the word.

The engines cut off and I watch as the airstrip staff put in place the steps to Fabio's jet. I'm not a patient man and I tap my foot, waiting for them to open the door. Finally, they open it, and a man appears at the top of the steps, shouldering a pink suitcase. I know instantly that it's the bodyguard Fabio said would accompany her for the handover. I insisted that none of her staff will remain her here in Boston. She will rely on my staff, who I know and trust.

The bodyguard descends the steps, and my fiancé comes into view. It feels like time slows the moment I set eyes on her. Aida shakes her long, dark brown hair out of her face as it blows in the wind, before glancing around. Her eyes land on me for a moment. I can tell, even though she is wearing sunglasses.

I watch with intrigue as she walks down the steps of the plane with a grace that surprises me. After the message I received from Fabio that his daughter wasn't too pleased about the arrangement, I half expected her to be dragged down by the bodyguard, kicking and screaming. Instead, she holds her head up high and barely looks at me.

I'm not used to women keeping their eyes off me the way she does. Once she makes it onto the concrete, she glances around as if trying to work out where she's meant to go.

I clench my jaw, wondering if this little virgin princess is trying to test my patience. She sets eyes on me, and they linger for a short while as she takes in my appearance. Unfortunately, the sunglasses hide her reaction to me. I feel irritated as she does another glance to ensure I'm the man she's here to meet.

Once she decides, she walks confidently toward the car without missing a step. I must admit I'm surprised by the confidence she exudes for a twenty-one-year-old woman who was flown across the Atlantic against her will.

She stops in front of the car, and I push off the hood, removing my sunglasses to get a good, close-up look at my property. I drag my eyes slowly down the sumptuous curves of her large breasts that are framed in a skin-tight pink cotton V-neck summer dress that dips low. Her hips are round and perfect for grabbing, and as I move my eyes back to her face, I admire her dark brown hair that cascades down to her waist. Also perfect for grabbing.

I feel my pants tighten at my crotch at the thought of breaking in this stunning virgin. There's no doubt that Fabio Alteri was modest about his daughter's beauty.

She clears her throat. "I assume you are Milo?" she asks calmly. It's as though I don't affect her at all, but that will change soon enough.

I memorize this cool and calm version of her, committing it to my memory. It won't be long until I shatter her calm into a million pieces before my eyes.

I turn my back on Aida and slip into the limousine without saying a word. She will learn in time that the only person asking questions around here is me. As I settle back into the Italian leather seat, I gaze out of the tinted window at her. She is standing on the tarmac, glancing around as if waiting to be told what to do.

James will ask her to get inside. I want to observe my new fiancé before I engage in any conversation. If she expects small talk, she'll never get it from me. I'm not one to indulge in pointless conversation.

James shuts the trunk and then speaks to Aida. "What are you doing, Miss Alteri?"

Aida shrugs.

He jolts his head toward the car. "Please get in."

I watch her, knowing she can't see me through the tinted glass. Her throat bobs as she stares at the door, looking uncertain about getting into a car with me. The woman is smart to be wary about entering enclosed spaces with me.

"Miss?" James encourages her to get in.

She only misses one more beat before walking confidently toward the door and sliding in opposite me. She pulls off her sunglasses and stows them in her bag. I keep my gaze on her, and she meets it, her dark brown eyes filled with enough confidence to stir an unexpected feeling inside of me—desire. A sensation that is often absent with the doormats I fuck.

I feel the tightness in my pants increase as my cock pulses against the zipper, wanting to break free.

My virgin is more beautiful and confident than I ever imagined. It will make breaking her in even more exciting.

Let the games begin.

3

AIDA

I jolt awake as the plane touches the ground. My vision is hazy as I open my eyes and my head pounds.

I notice Aldo sitting opposite me, and that's when it all comes flooding back. The clifftop where my father broke my heart in two. I never knew he could treat me with such cold indifference. The drugs Aldo pumped into me before the flight make my head swim as I rub a hand across my forehead.

In the space of one terrible day, my life has gone from blissfully carefree to one big nightmare that I can't wake up from. I groan as I lift my head from the headrest, as it feels too heavy for my neck. My father has fallen further than I ever could have imagined from the man he once was.

What would my mother think if she could see what he was doing to her only child?

My father always wished that they'd had a boy, but I never thought him heartless enough to sell me to such a cruel man. The mafia world is so dark and twisted. I know my father lost himself when my mother died. Ever since he lost her, he's clung to a greed that can never be satisfied.

Aldo clears his throat. "Your fiancé will meet you here. I must say goodbye to you now, Miss. Alteri."

My brow furrows. "Aren't you going to be my bodyguard here?" I ask. I don't understand why my father sent him on the plane with me if he will not stay.

He shakes his head. "Mr. Mazzeo's orders. None of your original staff will accompany you here."

I swallow hard, feeling panic claw at me. The thought of being thrust into that man's hands with no one I know makes this more daunting. Milo Mazzeo's infamous reputation is known far and wide. "Is there nothing you can do to convince him?"

Aldo shakes his head. "My life isn't here in America, Miss Alteri."

I grit my teeth as pain claws at my chest. Aldo never calls me Miss Alteri. He has been my bodyguard since I was about six years old and has always called me Aida.

"I see," I reply, glancing out of the window onto the runway where the plane taxis in. "And Mr. Mazzeo will meet me here?"

"Yes, he will." There's hesitation in Aldo's voice as he glances around. "You didn't hear me say this, Aida, but I'm so sorry this has to be your fate," he apologizes in hushed tones.

I meet his gaze, smiling as I look into his light blue eyes. "Thank you, Aldo. That means a lot to me." I shake my head. "My father has lost sight of what family means."

Aldo nods swiftly. "Indeed. You stay strong, and you will make it through this. I know you will."

I draw in a deep breath, trying to process his words. It's an odd sentiment since the rest of my life is about to be tied to a man so utterly irreparable. I'm not sure what I'm going to make it through. There is nothing to make it through for. All I know is that happiness is not what awaits me on that tarmac. Darkness and cruelty are about to become my reality, but I won't cower at the feet of a man who has secured my hand in marriage.

We roll past a limousine that has blacked-out windows. A young man stands by the door with it open, wearing a chauffeur's uniform. I glimpse a sight of someone getting out, but I don't get a good look at him.

The plane comes to a stop in front of a private airport. It's small, and there aren't many planes. Aldo stands and gathers my belonging strewn around the plane for me, placing them in my little pink suitcase. I gaze out of the window, trying to glimpse the man I'm due to marry.

"Are you ready?" Aldo asks.

I don't think I'll ever be ready to meet Milo Mazzeo, particularly not under these circumstances. I don't let my bodyguard know how scared I am and nod swiftly, holding my head up high.

The last thing I want Aldo to report to my father is that I left the plane kicking and screaming. Life in Boston is my fate, and I will face it with dignity, even if I am scared.

Aldo leads the way out of the plane and down the steps to the tarmac below. I slip my sunglasses on before stepping out into the fresh air and search for the man I'm due to wed. I notice him instantly, leaning against the hood of his limousine. I don't stare as I focus on the metal steps, walking toward my hellish fate with as much style as I can muster.

Aldo waits at the end and holds out a hand to help me off the last step. I take it, and he hands me my bag. "Keep in touch, Aida."

I grit my teeth to stop myself from getting emotional and give him a swift nod, taking my bag. Then, I focus my attention on the runway of the private airstrip. I scan it, making sure that the man standing by the limousine is indeed Milo. There's no one else here.

As I glance over at him and the car, I notice his jaw clench and shoulders tense. I glance one more time around the airstrip, wondering if this is irritating him. He stands a little straighter.

As I focus on him, my heart skips a beat. He wears an expensive, tailored navy-blue suit that fits him like a second skin. His dark brown hair is neatly styled with a side-swept fringe that falls across his right eye, and he has a neatly trimmed and groomed beard. I can't see his eyes, which are shaded by a pair of black sunglasses.

I can't deny that he is attractive. Still, if everything I've heard about him is true, his beautiful exterior is merely a wrapping for a rotten interior. He's a man who has no good inside of him.

I walk confidently toward the car. The driver is loading my cases into the trunk from the baggage handler. I clutch my handbag close to my side and wait for my fiancé to speak. Instead, he pushes off the hood of the car and removes his sunglasses.

I watch as he steps closer to me. His eyes are ice blue, and he slowly drags them down my body in the most predatory way. He doesn't speak as he moves his eyes back up my body with the same precise slowness, as if he's taking in every inch of me. It makes me feel naked. When his eyes meet mine, I'm thankful I'm wearing sunglasses. The intensity in his gaze scares me.

I clear my throat, trying to clear the tension from the air—tension that makes me sick to my stomach. "I assume you are Milo?" I keep my tone calm.

Milo stares at me for a few arduous beats before turning and getting into the car.

I don't follow since he hasn't said a word. The driver finishes placing the cases into the car's trunk before slamming it down with a thud.

"What are you doing, Miss Alteri?" he asks.

I shrug in response.

He nods his head toward the door. "Please get in."

I swallow hard, feeling uncertain about getting into the back of a car with that man—a man who can't even speak to me. He has no manners, but I'm not sure what I expected.

"Miss?" the driver pushes.

I hesitate for one moment before walking toward the door and sliding into the back of the limo.

Milo sits on the opposite side, staring at me with a look that sends shivers down my spine. He still doesn't utter a word as I pull my sunglasses off and stow them inside my handbag.

When I look back up, the intensity in his gaze is stronger. It feels like he is trying to intimidate me with all his quiet self-righteousness.

I stare back, wanting him to believe that I'm not some weak woman he can break. My father thinks I am, but he doesn't know me.

Milo has a reputation for cruelty, but I won't let that reputation scare me. Finally, he looks away and out of the window, giving me a moment's reprieve. He's an asshole for not speaking to me.

Why bother coming to meet me in the first place?

The driver slams the door of the limousine, making me jump. I notice a whisper of a smirk on Milo's lips at the first sign of fear from me. It irritates me more than I can put into words that I let a car door slamming shake me. The vehicle's engine starts, and I gaze out of the window, keeping my eyes off the man that won't even speak to me.

I have too much self-respect to ask him another question. The guy will not answer me. Instead, I dig my cell phone out of my handbag and check my social accounts. A sadness tugs at my chest when I see a selfie of Gia and Siena at the beach—a beach I'm never going to see again. It was our favorite place to hang out.

Gia and Siena were the only people on the island who didn't care who my family was. They accepted me, even though Aldo followed us around everywhere. And yet, my father didn't even give me a chance to say goodbye out of fear I'd try to run.

I sigh heavily, forgetting who is sitting opposite me. Perhaps I would have tried to escape given a chance. I can feel Milo's intense gaze burning a hole in me as I keep all my attention on my phone.

He's as much of a dick as I expected. At least he is attractive. I guess that's one positive I can take from this. That despite being married off to one of the cruelest men on the planet, at least he's easy on the eyes.

I almost laugh to myself at how ridiculous that is. There is no positive spin I can put on this utterly disturbing situation. My fiancé won't even say a word to me, and I can only assume that's because he wants to intimidate me. I hate the guy already, and he hasn't even said anything.

Will my hatred grow when he finally opens his mouth?

I feel that Milo not speaking to me is a blessing. So instead of letting it irritate me, I count myself lucky that he hasn't said a word yet.

If I'm lucky, I won't have to deal with him much since men like him are always busy with work. The briefcase of papers open on the seat next to him suggests he's just like my father, working every waking minute. The best I can hope for is that my husband has no time to torment me.

4

MILO

Silence cloaks the back of the limousine as I watch her intently, noting every quirk she has. It's rare that people regard me with such indifference. The entire time she keeps her head down, flicking through her phone. I can tell she is using it as a distraction, but not once does she glance out of the window.

It's clear her father was modest when he told me she was pretty. There's no world in which pretty is the correct word to describe the angel in front of me. Aida is stunning.

Her apprehension rolls off her in waves, but there's no fear. I expected her to fear me, but if she does, she's keeping it hidden. It's a conflicting sensation. I can't work out if her lack of fear excites or annoys me. Fabio's warning suggests she knows exactly the kind of man she was being married off to. So, why isn't she scared?

I'm not sure why I give a fuck. All I know is that the moment we say I do in four days, I'm going to break this beautiful virgin. The innocent woman that stepped foot on American soil only forty minutes ago will be unrecognizable by the time I'm done with her.

The limousine comes to a stop in front of my gates, and finally, Aida looks up for the first time.

Our eyes meet, and it feels like an electric shock pulses through my entire body. It's at that moment I realize I've stared relentlessly at Aida for the entire journey. Another human being hasn't held my full attention like that in my entire life. I clear my throat and look out of the window, finally tearing my eyes away from her. It's unlike me to be rattled by anyone.

James parks in front of my home, which Aida gazes at with indifference. I impress most women with my home when I bring them here on rare occasions, but my mafia princess is used to the high life. I dare say that Boston has nothing over the gorgeous shores of Sicily. Even as we come to a stop, she doesn't say a word or ask a question. It's a little unnerving, but perhaps she knows I have no intention of answering her questions.

I wait for James to open the door and help her out of the car. Aida doesn't even glance my way as she continues to stare at her phone, standing in front of my home. There's something different about this girl. I don't particularly appreciate that nothing is going the way I'd expected.

I clench my jaw and get out of the car, approaching

her from behind. It's impossible not to observe her beautiful figure. I can see over her shoulder that she's flicking through social media. Social media irritates me more than I can put into words, but I guess Aida, being fifteen years younger than me, has been pulled into the cult.

"Put your phone away," I order, standing so close to her she jumps.

I can't help but smirk at the satisfaction I feel. Deep down, she fears me, no matter how much she tries to hide it.

Aida spins around and meets my gaze with a confidence that I rarely see anyone look at me with. "Why should I?" She shakes her head. "We've spent forty minutes in a vehicle together, and the first words you say to me are 'put your phone away.'"

I narrow my eyes, surprised by her tenacity. "What did you expect from me?"

She glares at me with such fire in those dark brown eyes, I wonder if she has no fear at all. "Nothing." She turns her back on me and types on her phone again, explicitly defying my direct order.

Rage coils through me at the utter disrespect this girl has for me. I grab her shoulder hard, forcing her to face me. My other hand finds her slender throat, squeezing hard enough to shock her. For the first time, a flash of fear enters her deep, chestnut brown eyes. "Listen carefully, princess," I say, feeling the anger sparking out of control under the surface. Her eyes are full of burning hatred which was born before we met and stoked during the ride here. "I don't like disobedience. You're going to be my wife, and that means you'll do what I say when I say."

Aida tries to fight away from me, clenching her delicate fists and then beating my chest hard. I hold firm, unfazed by her attempt to get away from me.

I clench my jaw. "Do you understand?" I ask.

The feisty brunette merely glares at me. It's a look that makes my cock painfully hard in my boxer briefs. I don't like the unexpected, and my hungry desire for my fiancé is certainly unexpected.

Aida stops fighting against me, but the anger in her eyes remains. "Let go of me," she says calmly. Her calm only angers me further. She should be scared. Instead, she's ignoring my questions and being a spoiled brat.

I let go of her throat and capture her wrist tightly, yanking her toward my front door. Aida is playing with fire, pushing me the way she is. It's clear she needs to be taught how to respect the man who owns her. I intend to teach her a lesson, but not out here.

"Let go," she spits, fighting against me with all the strength she has.

I'm stronger, and I drag her toward the door, still fighting.

Piero opens the front door. "Sir, do you need help?" His eyes are wide as he looks at the feral woman I'm set to marry.

I shake my head. "No. Out of my way."

He steps aside as I drag Aida up the stairs toward her bedroom. It's become clear that she is going to make this hard on herself.

"You are embarrassing yourself, princess," I say through gritted teeth.

She stills against me. "Embarrassing myself?" Her voice is full of disbelief. "Do you think I care what anyone here thinks of me?"

I grind my teeth together as I reach the door of her room, right next to mine. "Open the door," I order, forcing her wrists toward the door.

"Open it yourself," she replies with hardly a moment of hesitation.

I growl softly. The irritation building inside of me is dangerous. Aida doesn't know the dark and depraved man she is messing with. All of this would have been easier if she'd just obeyed me.

I hold Aida's wrists with one hand and then force open the door with the other, pushing her inside.

I let go of her and shut the door, locking it behind us. The click of the lock is a violent sound. A sound that warns of what is to come. She's awoken the beast inside of me with her utter petulance. Our first meeting isn't going as I expected. I'm out of control and it's because of her.

I draw in a deep breath, trying to calm myself before turning to face my wife-to-be. "I think it's clear that we are going to have some serious problems if you don't learn to do as you're told, Aida."

She holds her head high, and the confidence in her eyes is both alluring and shocking. She's either fearless or willfully ignorant about the type of man she is dealing with—only time will tell which.

"Seems like it," she says, crossing her arms over her chest. "I'm not your possession. I'm a human being with rights."

I laugh at that. "Rights?" I shake my head. "Oh, Aida, you have no rights here." I step toward her, and for the second time, I see a flicker of fear in her chestnut depths—a fear I long to uncover. "You'll bend to my will because everyone does," I say, grabbing hold of her throat hard enough to partially block her airway. "Do you understand me?"

I hold her gaze, which despite my blocking her oxygen supply remains determined, even if the fear is present. She doesn't answer me or panic over my firm grip around her pretty little throat. I long to introduce this beauty to the darkest pleasures that warp my sick and twisted mind. Pain is something I relish doling out, whether or not the recipient is receptive. It doesn't matter to me.

I let go of her throat and grab both of her hips, spinning her around. Her firm, round ass presses into my crotch so she can feel how hard I am. "It's time for your first lesson, little virgin," I murmur into her ear, making her tense against me. For the first time, I've hit a nerve.

I force my fiancé toward the bed, and once the front

of her thighs hit it, I put pressure on her back.

She bends over the bed, and the skirt of her skimpy little summer dress rides up. I feel my cock pulsing against the strict confines of my boxer briefs and pants. Aida is wearing a little black thong that drives me insane. I pull the skirt of her dress higher, and she reaches around to pull it back down.

I spank her ass hard. "Don't move," I growl.

She squirms, and I realize the only way I'm going to stop her is if I tie her down. I link my finger through the loop of my tie and undo it before pulling her wrists roughly behind her back. Aida freezes as I wrap the silk fabric tightly around her wrists, binding her.

"What are you doing?" she asks, panic flooding her tone.

I grab hold of her hips once I've finished tying her binding. "I'm going to teach you a lesson, angel," I purr into her ear. I unbuckle my belt and pull it from my pants, folding it over in my hand. "Girls that don't obey need to be punished."

She remains silent and still in front of me. Aida doesn't beg me not to hurt her or tell me to stop. It's as though she's accepted her fate. I set my eyes on her creamy thighs and tight, round ass cheeks that make my cock hard as nails.

I grab her waist-length hair, forcing her to arch her back. "How does it feel to be at my mercy?" I ask, wanting her to break.

"Disgusting," she spits back, the fire in her voice still

as clear as before.

I growl softly, cupping her through the thin fabric of her thong. "Is that right? I bet you will be soaking wet like a needy little virgin by the time I'm through with you, princess."

Her thighs quiver at my attention, proving the effect I have on her. I bring the leather of my belt down firmly over her ass, making her yelp in pain.

"Next time, think again before you disobey me." I bring the leather down on her other ass cheek, staining it a deep red.

The sight of her at my mercy has more of an effect on me than I'd expected. Maybe it's because of her reluctance to be with me. This is the first time a woman I've encountered has stood up to me the way she's done.

It's a sick thought. I want Aida because she doesn't want me. My hands remain tight around my belt as I bring it down onto her ass again. Either she has gotten used to the pain or she's determined not to give me the satisfaction of reacting to my punishment. Aida remains entirely silent and eerily still throughout the rest of the harsh lashes.

I've never met a girl who can take pain so easily. There's no sign of her crying either, as she remains totally silent. I finish my punishment, standing back to witness my work. The satisfaction I feel at the deep red color of her skin is testament to how sick I am inside. The faint hint of blue bruising shows through her creamy skin, and it's more of a turn on than I can explain. I've marked Aida today, proving that she belongs to me. She will learn what that means soon enough.

Aida remains silent as I step forward and slide my finger under the string of her thong. It's soaking wet. I tease the tip of my finger through her virgin pussy, groaning since she is practically dripping.

The little virgin princess enjoys being punished, which makes walking away from her hard as hell. All I want is to bury myself deep inside of her, taking what I want from her without mercy. I draw in a deep breath, reining in my urges.

I untie the silk necktie from her wrists, knowing I must walk away. Aida remains bent over the bed, her pussy soaking wet and her ass red with welts. I walk away without a word, despite the beast inside of me recoiling against every fiber of my common sense.

I won't take her until we're married.

Piero is waiting in the basement with his arms crossed over his chest. He leans against the doorframe.

I stop next to him, glancing into the room where Luigi sits. The pool of blood under his chair irritates me, because I should have been the one to spill it. "Has he said anything yet?"

Piero nods. "He fucked up. Pure and simple."

I run a hand over my beard and narrow my eyes.

"You're certain he had no ties with the assholes that stole our drugs?"

"Very certain, sir. I tortured him thoroughly, but if you wish to continue, then there would be no harm in it."

I tilt my head to the side, looking at the piece of shit who lost me two-million dollars of cargo. "I'm not sure he'd withstand much more, Piero." I crack my neck. "I will finish this now; wait here."

Piero bows his head and leans against the wall outside of the room. My capo is the only man in this world that I truly trust. I'm not one for having friends. Life as a don of one of the most powerful organized crime groups in America is solitary, and I like it that way.

Luigi is half-dead, which irritates me. Aida impeded my work, but Piero did a good job in my absence. "You've cost me a lot of money, Luigi," I say.

His head snaps up at the sound of my voice. He squints at me through his busted-up eyes. "Sir, I'm so sorry, please—"

"Silence," I order, shaking my head. "I hate beggars, so keeping quiet is advisable."

Luigi shuts his mouth. I notice a wet patch stain his dark pants. This guy is an embarrassment to my organization, and I'm glad his fuck-up has weeded him out. I don't deal with a lot of the guys that work for me on a day-to-day basis. That's Piero's job.

I pull my knife out of the sheath on my belt and

approach him. "You cost the organization over two million dollars. Do you know what happens to people that lose me money?"

He can hardly look me in the eye. "They pay a heavy price."

I grab his throat hard and squeeze so he can't breathe. "It's not a heavy price to pay when you lose me money and then try to hide." I drag the knife across his arm, cutting him deeply. "You're a coward for not coming straight to me and explaining what happened." I let go of his throat. "Maybe if you had, I would have let you live." I tilt my head to the side. "Although, it's unlikely."

It's more likely that I would have killed him quickly with a bullet to the head. Instead, he's being tortured because he ran.

"Milo, please—"

I stab the knife into his leg forcefully, stopping his pathetic pleas. Instead, he squeals like the little bitch he is as blood paints the air. I must have hit the femoral artery, which will speed this process up.

"Do you think I'm a man who would give in to a plea for mercy?"

Luigi shakes his head, whining. "No, sir, but I've always been loyal to the Mazzeo family. I served your father—"

The mention of my father snaps the tenuous grasp I have on my control. I grab his throat hard to stop him from saying another word. "Don't fucking speak about my father." The rage inside of me is uncontrollable as I keep my hand tight around his throat.

Luigi's face pales as the blood drains from his body out of the major wound I inflicted. I slowly choke the life out of him, watching him fight for it. I enjoy the power rush it gives me, no matter how sick it sounds. There's nothing more exhilarating than taking away the life of someone who has wronged me.

I watch as he fights for his life harder than I expected, trying desperately to hold on. "Give up, Luigi. Death is your only path." I keep my hand clenched around his neck, feeling my wrist weaken slightly. The last tendrils of life slowly fade from his wide eyes as he slips into the afterlife. Once I'm sure he's gone, I let go and stretch out my wrists.

I'm angry when I see the splattering of blood on my white shirt. Piero will handle the body, so I leave the room. Piero is waiting outside, dutifully.

"It's done. Clean it up," I say, not waiting for his response as I walk out of the basement.

I walked into that room with the intention of slowly torturing him to death, but the firecracker I met at the airport had already tested my resolve. It's a bad omen. A sign that Aida is going to cause me more problems than she's worth if I can't get a handle on my urges. I need her to submit to me, but if our first interaction is anything to go on, it won't be easy.

I've always loved a challenge, but I can't understand why I feel so uneasy at the prospect of taming Aida.

5

AIDA

Pain clenches at my chest as I fight to draw breath into my lungs. I try to swallow the lump in my throat, wishing the tears would come, but they won't. I'm in shock.

I lie on my side as my ass hurts too much. My father's betrayal stings the most. He told Milo I'm a virgin, which is ammunition in the hands of a man like him. My husband-to-be is as terrible as I expected. It's probably why I'm not as surprised as I should be over what he did to me. It's everything I expected from him.

Milo locked me in this bedroom after spanking my ass and hasn't returned for hours. It's beyond boring and all I can do is drown in the emotional pain of everything that has happened. My cell phone rings, breaking me out of the trancelike state I'd fallen into.

I sit up, wincing at the pain as I grab it. My stomach

churns when I see Gia is video calling me. I wonder if she has heard what happened.

"Hey, Gia," I say, picking up the call.

She frowns at the camera, looking angry. "I can't believe you left for America without telling me."

I sigh heavily, knowing that her anger is not what I need right now. "I told you in my text that my father drugged me on the side of a cliff only an hour after I left the beach yesterday afternoon." I shake my head. "How was I supposed to say goodbye?"

"I always knew your dad was an asshole," Gia says, running a hand through her hair. "Hot, but also an asshole."

I wrinkle my nose, hating the way Gia calls my father hot. "He's not hot. He's my father. I've told you not to say that."

She laughs. "Sorry, Aida. It's the truth."

"Is that Aida?" Siena asks, coming into view of the camera. "How are you doing?"

I think about the question for a minute.

How am I doing?

I guess I've kept myself level-headed, considering my father had me drugged and shipped to a man who has no qualms about sexually abusing the woman he's engaged to. "Not great," I answer.

"What is your fiancé like?" Gia asks.

The mention of him angers me, even though I know Gia and Siena aren't aware of the man my father shipped me over to. They know runs the Sicilian mafia, but they aren't a part of the criminal world. "Horrible," I say, as it's the only word I can think of to describe him.

Gia's brow furrows. "Has he hurt you?"

I bite my lip, wondering whether or not to tell them how dire my situation is. Milo Mazzeo is the definition of evil. He has no morals. I mean, the guy laughed in my face when I told him I had rights. A shiver races down my spine as I remember the tone of his laugh.

"Aida?" Gia pushes.

I shake my head. "Not yet, no. He's not a nice man."

Gia sighs. "I'm half tempted to head to your house and tell your asshole of a father off for shipping you away."

My stomach twists at the thought. "Don't you dare, Gia. He's not a nice man either, and you don't want to piss him off." I'd hate to think what my father might do to Gia if she approached him. Most people that argue with my father end up dead or tortured, at least.

"I won't." She holds up her hands. "I don't understand why he'd do this to you."

That makes two of us. Ever since my mother's death, my father was more distant but always doted on me. He would take me out for special occasions and treat me often. I can't believe it was all a ruse to keep me close and sell me off when the time was right. "He told me I remind him too much of my mother."

Siena's eyes widen. "That's a terrible thing to say.

I'm so sorry, Aida. I wish we were there to help you through this."

"Can we come to the wedding?" Gia asks.

I shake my head. "I don't think he will allow it."

"Why not?" Siena asks.

My heart skips a beat as I hear footsteps nearing the door. "I've got a feeling someone is coming. I better go, guys."

Siena and Gia both look worried. "Keep in touch. We want to see you as soon as we're allowed to visit."

I swallow hard, knowing that might never be. "Of course. Bye." I cancel the call as Milo flings open the door.

He stands in the doorway with blood splattered on his shirt. He has no signs of injury, so it is someone else's. "You'll join me now for dinner."

I shake my head. "I'm not hungry." I meet his gaze, which looks a little psychotic. The things I've heard about him suggest he may well be.

"Who were you talking to?"

Shit. He heard me.

"Friends from Sicily."

He narrows his eyes. "I don't want you talking to anyone without me present. Do you understand?"

My brow furrows. "Why not?"

His square jaw clenches with frustration. He takes two steps into my room. "Let me be very clear with you, Miss Alteri. When I give you an order, you follow it without question. When I ask you to join me for dinner, you join me for dinner even if you aren't hungry. You know what I'll do if you disobey me, and next time I won't be so gentle."

I stare dumbstruck at the man I'm supposed to marry. "Gentle?" I stand from the bed, wincing as I bend over and lift my dress. "You call this gentle? I'm bruised and red-raw."

There's a low, beast-like growl behind me. "I wouldn't bend over like that if I were you, Aida," he warns, voice husky and raw.

I swallow hard and stand up, smoothing down my dress. The man I'm dealing with is as twisted as I expected.

Excitement pulses to life between my thighs at the thought of him punishing me again. It was oddly arousing, which makes me more disappointed in myself than I can explain.

"Fine, let's have dinner," I say, turning around and facing him.

His eyes are frantic with a mix of rage and arousal. The second emotion shocks me. There are a few moments as he stares at me like a madman in silence, and I wonder if I've pushed him too far. I don't know what it is about him ordering me, but I automatically get the urge to disobey him.

He breathes deeply and nods. "Follow me to the dining room." He turns around and walks stiffly out of the room. I follow him down the corridor and to the top of the stairs, which he descends. His home is similarly lavish to my father's home in Sicily. It's pretentious, but these men are all the same.

He leads the way down a corridor and stops in front of solid wood double doors, throwing them open to reveal a large dining room with an antique hardwood table in the center. I'm disappointed that he set the places next to each other rather than at opposite ends of the table. It means I have to spend dinner way closer to him than I am comfortable with, especially after what he did to me earlier.

Milo pulls out the chair to the right of the head place setting. "Sit."

I bite my tongue and sit in the seat without a word. Milo takes his seat, and almost on cue, a woman enters the room with a trolley and silver platters on it.

I watch as she brings the food to us. "Would you like me to serve you, sir?" she asks.

He shakes his head. "Leave us."

It appears he's as rude with his staff as he is with his future wife.

The lady bows her head before walking away and leaving me alone with this beast of a man. He stands and pulls the lid off the platter to reveal a rare steak. My stomach churns, and I realize my father hasn't told Milo that I'm a vegetarian.

He sets it in front of me.

"Milo, I can't eat this. I'm a vegetarian."

He seems surprised that I say his name. "It's sir to you." He moves the plate to his setting and then grabs another platter off the trolley and places it in front of me. "Your father didn't make me aware of your dietary needs, so dessert will have to be your only course."

I lift the lid on the platter, and my stomach rumbles at the sight of a gooey chocolate dessert. I'm a chocoholic, so I will not complain about chocolate for dinner. Not to mention, I've hardly got an appetite after everything I've been through in the past twenty-four hours. I'm exhausted and want to sleep.

Milo cuts into the rare steak, spilling blood all over his plate. The sight of it makes my stomach churn. My father loves steak, but I've seen no one eat it this raw, other than carpaccio, but that's thin slices, not the huge fillet he's tucking into. A heavy silence falls between us as I pick at my chocolate dessert.

I hate silence, but I've got too much pride to talk to him, knowing he will ignore me, anyway. Milo clears his throat. "Your father has sent the rest of your possessions by boat. They might be here in about two weeks. If there is anything you need, please let Olivia know. She will look after you." He doesn't look at me while he speaks, keeping his eyes on his steak.

"I've got everything I need," I say, spooning the dessert into my mouth.

Milo's jaw clenches at my response. "How about for the wedding?"

My stomach churns at the mention of our wedding. "What about it?"

He sets down his knife and fork with a clang and

levels his ice blue gaze on me. "Do you have everything you need? It's in four days."

My heart skips a beat. "Why so soon?"

His brow furrows. "Surely your father made you aware of the wedding date?"

I shake my head. "He told me nothing. Less than twenty-four hours ago, he drugged me and put me on a plane to Boston with no other information than that I will marry Milo Mazzeo."

An evil glint ignites in his eyes. "Your father is more ruthless than I could have imagined." He sounds unnervingly happy about it. "That's cold-hearted. Especially since this wedding date has been secured for two months now."

Two months? I drop my spoon and stare at him in shock. "Are you joking?"

Milo looks at me with a disinterested gaze. "Don't take your frustration out on me. I wasn't the one who didn't tell you for two months." He shrugs. "I thought it a little odd that your father didn't bring you to meet me sooner."

I feel a pain clutch around my heart. It's hard to hear that my father spent the last two months looking me in the eye and acting like everything was fine. All the while, he had sold me off to a man so cruel that his first impression on me was to spend a forty-minute car journey in silence before beating my ass.

"You're both as terrible as each other," I murmur.

He narrows his eyes. "You know nothing about me."

I laugh at that. "Everyone knows about you, Milo."

He grits his teeth, eyes blazing with a rage that scares me. "Don't call me Milo," he says through gritted teeth.

I should back off, but I raise a brow. "It's your name. You can't expect me just to call you sir."

He stands from his chair, making me jump.

I watch him like a hawk, knowing that this man has the power to hurt me in ways I can hardly imagine. A shiver races down the center of my spine as he walks behind me. It's impossible to remain relaxed, but I don't look at him as it would give him too much satisfaction. Instead, I keep my head forward, remaining calm.

He grabs my hair roughly, yanking my neck right back. Milo looms over me, trying to assert his dominance. I always knew that this would be anything but easy between us, but his desire to overpower me in every way is something I hadn't anticipated.

His ice-blue eyes are so cold as he stares down at me. "You will call me two names only, depending on what setting we're in." He laces every word with a threat. "When we are around others, you will call me sir. Let me hear you say it."

I glare up at him, keeping my mouth shut.

Milo grabs my throat with his other hand, squeezing so hard I can barely breathe. "Let me hear you say it," he drawls.

My pride is on the line, but as it feels like he might

choke the life out of me, I struggle to spit out the word. "Sir."

He releases my throat and nods. "Good. Next time, don't hesitate." He keeps his hand tight around my hair. "Whenever we are alone, I want you to call me daddy."

I swallow hard, an odd sensation pulsing to life between my thighs. Weirdly, the prospect of calling this cruel, dominant man daddy affects me. My inexperience is going to make dealing with Milo complicated.

"Let me hear you say it, princess," he purrs in a deep tone that makes my insides churn.

I can feel my cheeks blazing hot as I stare into his unforgiving eyes. Now I'm not defying him out of pride. I can't bring myself to call him daddy. It's too intimate and personal. It's the nickname a woman calls a man who protects and cares for her. Milo is the polar opposite.

"I want to hear you say it, Aida. Don't make me ask a third time." His other hand teases over my throat, warning me that he will block my airway if I don't say it.

I bite my lip, wishing I didn't have to call him that name. "Daddy," I whisper.

He yanks my hair harder. "Say it louder."

This man is well on his way to making me hate him more than anyone I've ever met in record time, and I've met some real assholes. "Daddy," I say louder.

He growls like a beast, grabbing my arm and

pulling me forcefully out of my chair. "Good girl. Now it's time for me to show you what that means."

I yank my arm from him, shaking my head. "I'm not some doll you can throw around." I cross my arms over my chest. "I'm a human being with rights, and before you tell me I don't have any, that's bullshit."

A cruel smirk curls onto his lips. "In my world, you don't." He grabs my wrist again and pushes me hard against the edge of the table, bending me over it.

I try to fight, but he's too strong.

"Time for daddy to taste his purchase," he murmurs behind me, pulling up the skirt of my dress.

"No, don't you dare," I reply.

He ignores me and pulls my panties down to my knees, leaving me bare.

The heat that spreads through me is a mix of sheer embarrassment and furious rage. "I said no. Don't you understand that word?"

Milo leans down over my body, biting the lobe of my ear. "That word is useless here, angel."

A shiver races down my spine as I realize I have no way of stopping him. I'm powerless and at his mercy. A fact that should scare me, but for some sick and twisted reason, it excites me. There must be something wrong with me, with the way my thighs get wet. It sickens me that I'm so easily turned on. I should have slept with Rinaldo, the boy I had a crush on for years, when I had the chance. Maybe then I wouldn't be so easily wound up by Milo's cruel touch. Rinaldo was a boy, but Milo is a man. A handsome man, not counting how ugly he is on the inside.

I feel his fingers teasing at the sensitive flesh between my thighs, and it sets me ablaze. No man has ever touched me. It's ridiculous how good it feels, especially since Milo doesn't care what I want. "Stop," I say, trying to break free from the tie he has tied around my wrists. "I don't want you to—"

He spanks my ass so hard I stop mid-sentence. "Liars get spanked. Your cunt is practically dripping for me. You want everything I'm giving to you and more." Before I can reply, I feel his face between my thighs as his tongue dips inside of the most intimate part of me.

"What are you—"

He spanks my ass so hard I yelp and then devours me like a beast. Every nerve ending in my body lights on fire as he relentlessly dips his tongue in and out of me. All thoughts escape me the moment he drags his tongue to my clit and licks me there over and over, pushing me toward release.

Milo parts my ass cheeks and then thrusts his finger deep inside of me. "So fucking wet," Milo growls behind me like an animal. "I know how much you want me."

I shake my head. "No, I don't," I respond, earning myself a thrilling spank that should hurt but only heightens my pleasure.

Milo hooks his fingers deep inside of me, hitting the spot that lights me up. I bite my lip, stopping myself from moaning out loud. It would give him too much satisfaction.

He digs his fingertips deeply into my bruised ass and licks me in the most intimate spot possible. I tense, wishing I could get away, but I'm trapped. His tongue probes at my back hole, and it's so dirty.

I grit my teeth. Everything this man is doing to me feels excruciatingly good. It's a struggle not to moan.

Milo spanks my ass again, and it's almost impossible not to squeal. I bite my bottom lip, feeling irritated that I made any sound at all.

"Your unnaturally heavy breathing has undermined your futile attempts to keep quiet." He spanks my ass again, increasing the unwanted pleasure he has invoked deep inside of me. "Now come for daddy," he growls, thrusting his fingers back inside of me and licking my throbbing clit in a way that sends me right over the edge.

No matter how much I try to fight it, I can't. My moans and whimpers frustrate me as much as the man plundering me with his fingers and licking me even as I come undone on his command.

It's embarrassing how easily he turned me into a moaning whore. Milo is the first man to touch me in such an intimate way, and I hate him for it.

6

MILO

I stare out of the window of my study, drinking my third glass of scotch. It's only ten o'clock in the morning, but I need something to get me through today. My wedding day. A day that I never thought I'd have to endure. It's a small price to pay since the business deal with Fabio Alteri will almost double our revenue.

"Are you ready, sir?" Olivia asks, lingering at the entrance to my study.

I knock back the rest of the scotch. "Almost. Is the car ready?" I ask, not looking at my housekeeper.

Olivia clears her throat. "Yes, James has already gone ahead with your bride. Piero is driving you today."

I turn and narrow my eyes. "Under whose orders?"

Olivia pales. "Piero suggested that because of the length of Miss Alteri's wedding dress, it was more practical for her to take the limousine, sir."

I grunt and wave my hand. "Fine. I'll be out in a minute."

She doesn't need to be asked as she leaves me in peace. I stare relentlessly at the family portrait my father had painted of us when I was a little boy.

Four days have passed since I met the woman I'm going to marry. Four days since I spanked her ass and made her come bent over my dining table. I haven't seen her again since our dinner together where things got out of hand. Olivia has looked after her, as I couldn't trust myself near her again until we marry.

There's a code we abide by with an arranged marriage, although I'm sure Fabio wouldn't give two shits if I fucked his daughter before the wedding day, especially considering he didn't care enough to accompany her. I know it's safer to abide by the rules of a deal. The last thing I want is to destroy a deal I've spent years trying to land.

I pour myself another small glass of scotch and knock it back before turning and leaving my study. Aida concerns me more than I'd voice to anyone. My reputation as self-assured in every choice I make is seriously on the line with my fiancé. I'm not sure marrying her is a good idea.

It would be easier if she didn't affect me the way she does. Her fiery defiance only makes me want her more. A sensation that I've never experienced before. Women are nothing more than an outlet for my urges. Normally one is not more alluring than another. However, Aida makes me lose control.

Piero stands next to his car, wearing a tuxedo. "How are you feeling, sir?" he asks as I approach.

I shrug. "Fine. It is nothing more than a business transaction." I clench my jaw at the lie, as it feels different to any business transaction I've ever done. We get into his car.

"How have you got on with her up to now?" Piero asks, turning the key in the ignition.

I glare at my capo as he knows I don't like small talk. "Not well."

He nods. "I guess it's expected since the girl has been uprooted from everything she knows and thrown into a situation she has no control over." He pulls out of the gates of my home, heading toward the church.

He's right. Aida has been through a lot, but her defiance suggests that the situation hasn't affected her in the way I expected. She is strong, and that's not what I want from a wife. A doormat would be a lot easier.

I glance at my capo, who drives with such calm in my presence. He's probably the only man that is relaxed around me. "She is very disobedient." I run a hand across the back of my neck. "For a girl who should be scared, she sure as hell doesn't act like it."

Piero smiles. "Don't you know the disobedient ones are always the most fun?" He sounds like he's talking from experience, but I don't know that. Any woman I've been with has been a doormat. They haven't challenged me the way Aida challenges me.

Piero parks the car around the corner from the church. He gets out and goes to open my door, but I exit before he can. My capo doesn't need to act like my chauffeur.

"I haven't been in a church since I was about this high," he says, signaling about a meter above the floor.

I nod. "Makes two of us."

He lets me walk in front of him to the entrance of the church. My uncle is already here, which is irritating. We don't exactly get on, but he is my only living relative —it would have been disrespectful not to invite him.

The small Catholic Church entrance is ornate, and people I don't wish to see chatter in front of it as if this is a joyous occasion. My heart skips a beat when I see Carmella, my ex. She's also the daughter of one of my rivals. No one invited her, which makes her presence an underlying threat.

I grab Piero's shoulder and make him aware. "Carmella is here," I hiss.

"Don't worry, sir. I'll monitor her."

It's impossible not to worry when Donatello is messing with a day like this. I nod anyway, knowing I can trust Piero to keep an eye on her. Piero steps aside so I can move further into the church to take my position at the end of the aisle.

I half expected the whole place to burst into flames the moment I step foot inside the walls. I haven't been to a church since I was a little boy. Aida was brought up catholic, and it was one of Fabio's wishes that she marries traditionally.

If it had been up to me, we would have done this in a local registry office with one witness. All I want is to get this over and done with and then return to life as usual after our honeymoon. I won't allow Aida to change my way of life.

All the guests take their seats, including my ex. I can't believe she's here at my wedding. The string quartet plays the wedding march. I glance down the aisle to see Aida at the entrance with a veil shielding her face. The white wedding gown she wears frames her luscious curves flawlessly.

This is the first time I've seen her since things got out of control at dinner the first day she arrived. A flood of desire pulses through me the moment I set eyes on her again.

Aida holds her head up high as she always does, approaching me at a slow pace. She's entirely alone as she walks down the aisle, but she has a confidence that is impossible not to admire. Piero stands to my left-hand side, clutching the rings. The thought of wearing a wedding ring permanently makes my skin crawl, but it's a tradition which I'll indulge for now.

Aida stops opposite me, keeping her head bowed. I reach for the veil over her face and lift it, revealing her beauty. It kicks me in the gut all over again. Aida's more stunning than I can put into words.

Her chestnut brown eyes hold that irritated fire as she stares at me with passionate hatred. An emotion I can work with.

The priest starts the ceremony, but I don't listen. His words mean nothing to me, as I'm beyond retribution. I never had faith to begin with, and after everything I've been through in my life, I will never find it. Instead, I memorize every blemish and detail of Aida's face, waiting for the moment this is finally over.

"Milo, do you take this woman to be your lawfully wedded wife?" the priest asks.

I meet her gaze, and the challenge in them only excites me. "I do." There's no hesitation in my voice, despite my apprehension earlier.

The priest looks satisfied and glances at Aida. "Aida, do you take this man to be your lawfully wedded husband?"

She glares at me hatefully, and the silence ticks by as she hesitates. If she thinks saying no now will get her out of this, then she is mistaken. The priest knows that there might be some resistance, but he is to marry us, anyway.

After a painfully long pause, Aida finally speaks. "I do."

I feel an odd satisfaction that she doesn't fight the inevitable. I hold my breath, waiting for the order from the priest.

"I now pronounce you husband and wife. You may kiss the bride," the priest announces.

I search Aida's eyes, which ignite with a deep irritation. An irritation that only fuels the desire inside of me. I wrap my arms around her waist and pull her close. She tenses against me, glaring at me with a hatred that stirs more desire inside of me. Her eyes search mine for a shred of regret for what I did to her the other night, but she won't find it.

I meld my lips to hers forcefully and slide my tongue into her mouth. She nips at my tongue with her teeth in a warning, but all it does is make me want her more. I growl softly into her mouth, not caring who is watching us.

She tries to fight me, setting her hand on my chest and pushing at me. I know that people watching will detect her resistance, but I don't give a shit. When I finally break the kiss, she glares at me with flushed cheeks.

I hold out my arm to her, which she reluctantly takes. We walk down the aisle, and I notice Carmella is no longer in her seat. Concern floods me, and I glance around the church. My eyes stop when I notice Lorenzo, her father's henchman, lingering in the side wings. Tension coils through me like poison spreading to every inch of my body. Adrenaline pulses through my veins, and I know my wedding is about to turn into a bloodbath if I don't act.

Casually, I move my gaze across all the guests. If Lorenzo realizes that I've noticed him, he might act quicker. I lean toward Aida and whisper into her ear,

"When we get to the door, I want you to run to James and tell him to call Antonio. Do you understand?"

Aida meets my gaze with confusion, but it's as if she knows from one look that I'm not messing about. "Yes." Her throat bobs as she swallows. Aida will be used to danger around every corner, considering who her father is. Time slows as we make the last few steps to the door of the church. My heart is pounding hard in my ears as she lets go of my hand.

I watch her move gracefully and fast down the church steps while I pull my gun from my inside jacket pocket. The move earns a few gasps as I spin around and aim it at Lorenzo. He sees the move coming as I pull the trigger, missing him as he ducks behind a column. "Everyone vacate the church immediately," I call.

A frantic rush of people flee the church. Luckily for me, all the guests at the wedding ceremony know the true nature of my business. Piero joins me, pulling his gun as well. "How many are there?" he asks as the few men in attendance rally by my side.

I shake my head. "All I know is that Lorenzo Ricci is here, and so is Carmella. I don't know where she's gone."

Lorenzo shoots at me from the other side of the pillar. The bullet grazes my neck as it passes a mere millimeter short. "Motherfucker," I growl, darting behind the nearest column.

Piero follows suit, taking cover behind the opposite

column. Brando Donatello will pay for this, attacking me at my wedding. Four more of my men attended the wedding, and they are all ready for a fight. Elio, Paolo, Tore, and Sergio. They will all put their lives on the line to make sure none of Donatello's men leave this church breathing.

The shots ring out again, bounding off the stone pillars. Lorenzo has two men with him, which means he's outnumbered. Not to mention, he's backed into the church with no escape.

"Surrender now, Lorenzo, and maybe I'll make your death quick," I shout, glancing around the pillar.

He pops up from the pew he's hiding behind and shoots at me. "Never."

Tore fires a shot at him and misses. He doesn't notice one of Donatello's men to the left. I don't have time to warn him as he's shot in the shoulder. "Merde," Tore shouts, clutching his arm.

The guy was so focused on Tore, he didn't keep an eye on me. I bring my gun up and shoot the guy in the head, killing him with one shot. "One down. You're outnumbered and have nowhere to go. What's your plan?"

Lorenzo is silent. He doesn't have a plan, since it's already gone to shit. Lorenzo had intended to catch us all by surprise, but I saw him first. It wouldn't surprise me if he planted a bomb in the church, which doesn't bode well. If he thinks there's no way out, then he might set it off, anyway.

Lorenzo fires a shot at Elio, who is trying to draw him out. "The police will be here soon," Lorenzo shouts back. "You won't have time to kill me and make an escape."

I focus my attention on the sirens in the air, cursing under my breath.

Piero shoots toward the pillar and then steps out from the column, shooting as he moves across to join me. "What's the plan, boss?" He meets my gaze with a calculating calm amid chaos. This is a perfect example of why this man is my second in command. He's one of the few men I can trust to think quickly and handle the unexpected.

Donatello's attack was unexpected but not unbelievable. He's wanted me dead for years. I shake my head, feeling irritated that I won't have time to kill that son of a bitch, Lorenzo. Brando has always had a chip on his shoulder since I dumped his whore of a daughter when I was nineteen years old. He and my father were business partners, but that ended badly when my father crossed him.

Carmella was my one and only girlfriend. I ended it when I walked in on her fucking my high school friend and vowed I'd never commit to a woman again.

Brando believed his daughter that I'd been the unfaithful one and resisted killing me only because of his deal with my father. My marriage to Aida will be different, though. If she dares to lay with another man,

I'll kill him and make her watch before locking her away for the rest of her miserable life.

"Sir?"

I grit my teeth and listen as the sirens grow closer. If we stay too long, the police will be here before Antonio's backup. We need to get out of here before it's too late. "Antonio will not make it on time." I shake my head. "We don't have time to wait."

Piero nods. "They're almost on us. We'll make a plan to strike back at that piece of shit, Donatello." He glances over at the rest of the men who keep firing rounds when they get a chance, whistling. He signals them out.

I go first, backing out of the church and shooting as I do. My men do the same, dodging bullets as Lorenzo and his sidekick try to catch us off guard. I make it out, followed by Piero and the rest of my men.

The last man to make it to the door is Sergio, but he gets shot. "Fuck," he shouts, clutching his abdomen and leaning on the outside of the church for support.

Tore lends him a hand. It's a flesh wound, but it will need to be treated. None of my men can attend a hospital considering the type of injuries they have sustained. It means they have to return to my estate for medical treatment, which isn't ideal considering hundreds of guests are turning up for the wedding reception.

Once outside, I issue the order fast. "Everyone, back to my estate now," I shout, rushing to Piero's car.

My men act fast and get into their vehicles, too.

Piero unlocks his Mustang, and I jump inside. The engine's roar is satisfying as Lorenzo and his man rush out of the church, firing bullets at us. They are too late.

"Stronzo," Piero curses as the bullets ricochet off his Mustang—a car he loves more than anything in this world. "I'll have all of their heads on a fucking spike for that," he growls as he races away from the church down the main road, taking a left to get off it. "We'll take the back roads. It's safer. That way we can ensure there's no ambush waiting for us and the police don't catch us."

"Sounds good to me," I reply, loosening the tie around my neck. I knew my wedding day would be fraught, especially marrying a woman who didn't want to marry me, but it's gone worse than I expected.

Time to get this reception over with, since I've been looking forward to what follows ever since Aida stepped off that plane onto US soil. Tonight, the little virgin is going to become mine in every sense of the word.

7

AIDA

My head spins as I rush down the steps of the church, wondering if my life is in danger. It wouldn't be the first time and no doubt not the last. The moment I heard the warning in Milo's voice, I knew not to question him. It took me right back to the day my mother died. My father told me to run then, and I did, only to glance back and see a man shoot my mother through the head.

James is standing by the limousine, and he glances up, eyes widening in surprise. "What's going on?"

I shake my head. "I don't know. Milo whispered to me as we walked out of the church to run to James and tell him to call Antonio."

He tries not to look shaken, but the panic is clear in his eyes as he opens the door to me. "Get in, Aida."

I do as he says, sliding into the back of the vehicle.

He slams the door behind me and gets into the driver's seat, starting the vehicle.

After being brought up around danger, I'm no stranger to this kind of panic. It's second nature to me, and I know not to ask questions in the middle of a tense situation.

James drives away from the church, taking a different route back. He is on the phone in seconds, on speaker.

"Antonio, Milo needs back-up at the church right away."

The man on the other end has a poor signal and is a little muffled. "What happened?" he asks.

I can see James shaking his head. "No idea. They have given me instructions to get his wife away and to call you."

"Okay, on my way." He cancels the call.

"Do you know what's going on?" I ask as silence falls between us.

James clears his throat. "I know less than you. I'm sure Mr. Mazzeo and the other guests will join us back at his home for the reception."

I sit back in the seat and watch the concrete jungle racing past the window. Other than the journey from the airport to Milo's home, this is my first time outside. Boston is certainly different from Sicily, with its modern buildings crammed into every available inch.

I'm a world away from the ancient stone villas sweeping across the hills and mountains of my home country. I miss it more than I can put into words. Danger is a part of this world, but I feel Milo is a magnet for more of it than my father was.

I'm not surprised after my few dealings with him up to now. He's an asshole. The kind of man that makes enemies by being himself. After the way he treated me, he's the first person I've ever truly hated.

James glances in the rearview mirror. "How are you holding up?"

I shrug. James is the first person to ask me how I am or treat me like a human being since I landed in America, except for Olivia, Milo's housekeeper. "I'm fine. I think it's a blessing that I've got time away from my husband."

James meets my gaze again in the mirror, eyes wide. "Don't let Mr. Mazzeo hear you say that."

I shake my head. "I'm not scared of him."

He clears his throat. "You should be, Aida. He's not the kind of man you want to piss off."

I clench my jaw and stare out of the window, ignoring his warning. Deep down, I know he's right. Milo is cruel.

When he kissed me after the priest pronounced us man and wife, he was forceful despite my reluctance. He didn't care that I didn't want his tongue shoved down my throat in front of about forty people. Everything I've learned up to now tells me that consent isn't something he's big on, and probably less so now that we're married.

I dig my cell phone out of my bra and check my texts. Ever since I got here, my father hasn't bothered to contact me. I've gotten messages from Gia and Siena wishing me luck with my wedding. It sucks that they couldn't be here by my side.

I swallow hard as I think about all the silly expectations I had about my wedding. For a start, I expected to be in love with the man I married. Second, I expected my father to walk me down the aisle. Third, I was sure my two best friends would have been with me throughout the day.

None of my expectations came true, and I feel a deep sadness that I'll never get my dream wedding. It's something many girls dream of. Reading fairytales taught me my prince charming would come along. Instead, I've been given away to a villain.

James pulls up the drive of Milo's mansion. There are lots of cars in front of it. "Why so many cars?"

"The wedding reception guests. Milo is an important man in this city, and he invited anyone important."

I hug my arms around myself at the thought of having to meet people and be pleasant. "I assume they aren't aware of Milo's profession?"

James shakes his head. "No, of course not." He laughs. "Do you think the mayor of Boston would be here if he knew Milo runs the criminal underworld of his city?"

Milo must be a big deal then if the mayor bothered to attend his wedding reception. It's hard to believe that the elite are so blind to the people they're mixing with. In Sicily, the police and the government are as corrupt as my father. They know what he does. They choose to take his money and look the other way.

"Surely they will find it strange that Milo and I had an arranged marriage."

James turns off the engine and glances in the mirror. "Didn't Milo tell you what to say to people?"

I shake my head. "He hasn't told me anything."

James sighs. "He probably intended to fill you in on the journey from the church. Don't tell people it was an arranged marriage and be vague if you get questions about your relationship." He pulls his cell phone out and checks it. "They've fled the church now and are on their way here. You won't have long until Milo joins you."

I don't know whether or not to be thankful for that. On the one hand, the thought of facing hundreds of important people from this city inside all by myself fills me with dread. On the other, I'm not sure having Milo by my side would put me at ease.

James gets out of the car and opens the door to me. "Don't look so worried. I'm sure you will be fine." He holds his hand out to help me.

I take it as he has been nice—nicer than anyone else up to now. "Thanks." I smile.

"No worries. Keep smiling, bella. It's your wedding day."

My stomach sinks at his words. It's almost impossible

to keep smiling. As a little girl, I dreamed about my fairytale wedding. Fairytales certainly aren't real, and I'm in the opposite of one. I stare up at the enormous mansion.

It's a daunting scene as people flood through the entrance. I know no one in there, and the man I've married is nowhere to be seen. This should be fun. I reluctantly walk to the entrance and enter. Guests stare at me as I make my way toward the ballroom, hoping there aren't too many people already in there.

Somehow, I've got to avoid speaking to anyone until Milo gets here. It makes me wish more than anything that Gia and Siena were here. Instead, they're probably enjoying themselves at our favorite beach outside Palermo or enjoying the day shopping. I long to be back in the beautiful country where I grew up.

My eyes widen as I see how many people are in the ballroom. There must be at least three hundred people at this reception, maybe more. It's surprising that Milo has any friends or acquaintances at all after his impression he made on me.

I grab a drink from one of the waiters walking by before slipping toward a quiet corner of the ballroom. It will not be easy to blend in wearing this stunning A-line wedding dress. Maybe I'm paranoid, but I feel like everyone's attention is on me.

A man locks eyes with me and smirks, approaching. "You must be the bride," he says.

I raise my eyebrow. "What gave me away?"

He laughs. "I'm Michael. It's a pleasure to meet you, beautiful." He takes my hand forcefully and presses his lips to the back of it. He's trying to be charming, but it's coming off creepy. "Aida," I reply, wishing that he hadn't come over here as I reclaim my hand from his grasp.

He's young, probably in his late twenties, and smells too strongly of overpowering men's cologne. "You're not originally from America, are you?"

I swallow hard, shaking my head. "No, I'm from Sicily."

"Exotic and attractive. I can see why Milo picked you."

My brow furrows at the rude comment. "Excuse me?"

He shrugs. "It's a compliment, beautiful."

I can hardly believe the nerve on this guy. He's hitting on me at my wedding. "You realize that I've just gotten married, right?"

He leans closer to me, touching my arm gently. "I love married women. They're always kinkier."

I jolt away from him, shocked by the way he shamelessly flirts with a bride at her wedding reception. "In your dreams."

He looks irritated by my comment, but then his attention goes elsewhere, and he steps away from me. I'm thankful for the distance until I see why he stepped away.

Milo approaches us with a possessive rage in his gaze.

Michael addresses him, "Milo, I was getting to know your new wife."

I notice Milo's jaw clench as he slips an arm around my waist without looking at me. He pulls me possessively against the side of him, holding me tightly.

He fixes all his attention on the creep that propositioned me at my wedding reception. I still can't believe that he was serious. The look on Milo's face could kill, and it wouldn't surprise me if he wanted to kill Michael for touching his wife.

My husband is a dangerous man, but from the cocky glint in Michael's eyes, he does not know who he's messing with.

8

MILO

Fiery rage infects my blood as I sit in the passenger's seat of Piero's car, watching ahead as he pulls into my driveway. There are lots of cars parked out front, making it impossible to get close. A wedding reception is underway without the groom.

All I want right now is to turn the fuck around and find Brando Donatello. He needs to pay for making me look weak, attacking me at my wedding. The wedding reception makes it impossible to do anything right now. People would notice if I were absent, but I will make him pay for attacking me. Ironically, I'm attending my wedding reception with politicians and Boston society's elite after being involved in a shoot-out.

No one knew where the wedding was taking place, other than my men, some business associates, and my family. It begs the question of how Brando Donatello found out where it was. There's a traitor for sure, one that will need to be weeded out.

For now, I must socialize and act like I care about the charities Patricia, the mayor's wife, is touting. As one of the richest men in Boston, I am forced to associate with politicians and socialites. If I were to marry without inviting the city's elite, there would be a lot of chatter—chatter I've made it my mission to avoid.

I glance over at Piero. "Antonio is meeting us here, isn't he?"

Piero nods in response. "Yes, he'll deal with Tore's and Sergio's injuries in the guest house."

"Good. We can't have word of this getting around the guests. Make sure it all goes smoothly."

Piero parks in front of the house, keeping the engine running. "Of course, sir. Have a good time."

I roll my eyes. "You know I'd rather be doing anything than mixing with these people."

"Yes, but you have to act like you're having a good time, at least."

I clench my jaw, knowing that, unfortunately, Piero is right. "See you later." I get out of the car, and he drives toward the guest house. Piero will deal with my men and make sure no one sees them. I'm confident of that. I adjust my jacket and walk through the entrance into my home.

Jackson, a city council member, spots me first. "Milo, congratulations on the wedding." He shakes his head. "I didn't even know you were dating."

I clear my throat, drawing in a deep breath. "It was a whirlwind romance," I lie. The fact that I've never entered society with my now wife will have already caused quite a stir amongst the gossipers.

Jackson's brow furrows. "Where is she?" he asks.

"She went on into the ballroom, I believe." I glance in that direction. "I best find her."

He opens his mouth to say something else, but I walk away before he can. The guy is irritating, and I know it will look weird that I'm not by my bride's side. Not to mention, I haven't filled her in on our cover story. Hopefully, she hasn't had conversations with anyone important.

I walk toward the ballroom, searching for my wife. Aida stands to one side, talking to Michael King, a young and rich businessman renowned for hitting on everyone else's wives.

Rage slams into me as he leans toward her suggestively, the distance between them shortening. I won't stand for another asshole making me look a fool on my wedding day.

My attention remains fixed on the two of them as I approach. The moment Michael notices me, he steps away from my wife. "Milo, I was getting to know your new wife." There's a glint in his eyes that makes me want to knock him out right here in front of everyone.

I slide my arm around her waist and pull her close. "I'd stay away from other people's wives if I were you, Michael. You know what happened the last time."

Michael laughs as if I'm joking. If he only knew the kinds of things that I'd do to him if he ever placed a hand on my wife, he would run. "I'm only talking to your bride, Milo. There's no need to get defensive."

I stare at him with a frosty glare. "Talk to someone else. I need a moment with my wife."

He holds his hands up. "Fine. It was nice to meet you, Aida." He walks away, glancing back at Aida briefly.

"That guy is a creep," Aida says, watching after him too.

"Did he touch you?"

Aida's brow furrows as she meets my gaze. "What does it matter if he did?"

I growl softly and pull her close, angling her chin upward. "I'd kill him if he did. If any man other than me ever lays a hand on you in that way, I'll kill them. Do you understand?"

She pales slightly at the intensity in the sentiment. I'm not sure whether it's a sentiment entirely driven by possession. All I know is that the thought of another man going near her drives me insane. "Yes, sir," she whispers.

It's the first time she has willingly addressed me like that, and all my blood rushes south in response. "Good girl," I purr into her ear before kissing a path across her jaw to her lips. "I can't wait to show you what you've been missing, little virgin," I whisper, biting the lobe of her ear. "I bet you're so wet thinking about it."

CRUEL DADDY

She pushes me away, glaring at me with that fiery hate. "You're a pig," she says, only loud enough for me to hear. The woman is smart. She knows not to make a scene in front of these guests.

I smirk at her. "I know you want me. There's no use denying it."

Someone clears their throat behind us, drawing my attention. "Milo, I believe congratulations are in order," the mayor, Thomas Allinson, says.

I straighten my posture and slip my hand onto Aida's back. "Thank you, Thomas. May I introduce you to my wife, Aida."

He smiles at her and takes her hand, shaking softly. "It's lovely to meet you, Aida." He glances at me. "Odd to be meeting her as your wife for the first time, though."

I shrug. "We fell in love on my trip to Sicily two months ago, and we couldn't wait to make it official. I'm sorry we didn't do introductions sooner."

Aida tenses against me as I mention our backstory. A story I've yet to fill her in on.

He waves his hand dismissively. "These things happen."

His wife, Patricia, approaches, her eyes fixed on me as they always are. She's tried to get me to fuck her on many occasions, but I avoided her advances.

"What are you talking about?" she asks.

I smile at her. "I was introducing your husband to my new wife, Aida." I glance at Aida, who looks uncomfortable as Patricia glares at her like the jealous bitch she is.

"Oh, wonderful to meet you," she says with absolutely no sincerity. "Shame we couldn't have attended the ceremony."

Thomas nods. "Yes, I'm sure you could have had space for the mayor and his wife."

I grit my teeth. "We both wanted a small and intimate ceremony with just family and close friends." I level my gaze at Michael. "I'm sure you can understand the desire for privacy with the public life you lead."

Thomas laughs. "You always are so private, aren't you, Milo?" He shrugs. "Never mind. We're glad we could come and celebrate with you at least." Thomas lifts his glass and clinks it against mine as I stare at the snake that runs this city.

It's pathetic how blind and stupid they are. "Yes, thank you for coming," I reply, tightening my grip on Aida's hip. "We must greet our other guests."

Thomas nods. "Of course."

I guide Aida away from him, knowing that spending too long in his presence is never a good idea. Thomas is too curious about my businesses and operations in the city. I know he doesn't suspect who I am, but he doesn't like that I'm so private.

"That's the story we are telling people?" Aida asks, only loud enough for me to hear.

I glance at her. "Yes, we met two months ago in Sicily. Simple."

Aida raises a brow. "How did we meet?"

I clench my jaw. "We don't need specifics."

Aida shakes her head. "You realize that's one of the most common questions anyone asks. They want the story of how the couple met."

I yank her forcefully into a small nook off the ballroom, away from prying eyes and big ears. "Stop questioning me, Aida."

She meets my gaze with that fire that makes me want to strip her down and fuck her right here in the middle of our reception. "I don't want to get anything wrong."

I breathe deeply and nod. "Fine. We met through your father, who was an acquaintance at a party I was invited to. Once we were introduced, it was clear we felt something for each other, and the rest was history."

Aida looks a little bemused that I answered her. "Okay."

I dig my fingertips into her hips, hard. "Okay, what?" I ask.

The tip of her tongue darts out over her luscious pink lips, drawing my attention to them. "Okay, sir."

I shake my head. "We're alone, princess. I want to hear you say it."

Her cheeks flush a deep red, and she glares at me with a dark hatred. A hatred that stirs more desire inside of me than it should. "No. You said when we're alone, and we're not alone." She shakes her head.

"We're in a room with about five hundred other people, for fuck's sake."

I grab her throat hard enough to warn her I'm serious and tease my lips along the edge of her jaw. "Remember what happens to naughty girls that don't obey. I won't hesitate in punishing you right here where everyone can hear you cry."

Aida shudders against me, eyes dilating as she meets my gaze. Every time I assert my dominance over her, she gets turned on. "Okay, daddy," she says with a sultry tone that makes my cock harder.

I let go of her throat and grab her hand, forcing it over the crotch of my pants. "Good girl. Daddy is so hard for you, princess."

She tries to pull her hand off my cock, but I hold it there.

"So hard and ready to fuck that pretty little virgin cunt of yours," I purr into her ear softly before allowing her to let go of my cock. "Now come and be a good little wife and help me greet our guests."

Aida glares at me with passionate hate, but there's something else in her gorgeous eyes. Desire—desire to have my cock buried deep inside of her.

I don't have long to wait. By the end of the day, Aida will no longer be a virgin. I will take her and turn her into my submissive little slut to do with as I please.

9

AIDA

"We'd like the happy couple on the dance floor for their first dance," someone says over the microphone, making my stomach churn.

"The happy couple" is the most laughable thing I've heard all day. The thought of dancing with that man in front of these people makes me feel sick.

My heart rate picks up as Milo stalks across the room toward me. His eyes are pinned to me as I try not to meet his gaze. He slips his hand onto my lower back and leans toward my ear. "Time to make our relationship believable, angel."

I hate him calling me angel, but what I hate more is the way my thighs quiver when he does. It's as though I have no control over my urges—urges that make no sense. Milo has been an asshole to me since I arrived. He's the last man on this earth I should want, and yet a dark, twisted part of me wants him to take me roughly despite my pleas for him to stop.

"Unfortunately, that's virtually impossible," I reply.

Milo shakes his head. "Bullshit. I know how badly you want me."

His cockiness makes my skin crawl as I try to fight the conflicting feelings raging inside of me. "Let's get this over and done with," I mutter.

Milo leads me onto the dance floor of the vast ballroom in front of the hundreds of guests. The band starts to play a traditional Italian song. "Follow my lead."

I blink at him once before he suddenly whisks me into the tango. My heart skips a beat as I miss my step and stand on his foot.

He doesn't bat an eye, continuing through the moves as if he was born to dance—a skill I never expected him to have.

I fall into step, matching his moves. My father paid for my dance classes for years, but he never let me go out dancing with my friends. This is the first time my skills have been used.

Milo holds my gaze as we dance with an intensity that could boil my blood. Trust him to choose the most passionate dance. He moves with elegance as his dark gaze burns a hole into my soul.

It's hard to draw breath into my lungs as he spins me around and pulls me into his body, swaying me to the music. The hard press of his cock evident in his suit pants against my ass. A blazing heat sweeps through my body as desire pools between my thighs. Milo's hand teases down the side of my body and then back up again before he spins me around to face him.

It's as though we're the only two people in the room. My anxiety over being watched melts away. My husband guides me without hesitation across the dance floor, never once missing a step. It's irritating that part of me wants to give in to the dark desire buried within. Part of me wants Milo to take my virginity tonight with no mercy, tying me down if he wants. Not that I'd admit that out loud to him.

Milo pulls me close, wrapping his leg around mine in a way that presses me harder into him. He lingers in this position for a few beats longer than he should, whispering into my ear, "I'm going to dip you to finish. Brace yourself, angel."

I find it odd that I trust him to dip me or lift me during this dance. The way he holds me promises he won't let me go, even if he will take pleasure in hurting me later. The music crescendos and I wrap my leg around him as he dips me down, holding my weight as I arch toward the floor.

The guests erupt into cheering the moment the music stops.

Milo pulls me close to him. Both of us breathe heavily as we stare into each other's eyes. "I can't wait to tango with you in the bedroom, angel," he murmurs, kissing my lips hard.

I tense initially on instinct, but the six glasses of champagne I've drunk since I arrived at the reception have lowered my inhibitions. Milo's tongue delves into my mouth—demanding submission from me.

I give in to him, leaning closer as his tongue plunders every inch of my mouth. He's like a beast devouring me in front of our guests. Milo doesn't care who is watching. His fingers dip into my hips hard enough to bruise as the passion in his kiss increases.

I hate this man, but I want him all at the same time. It makes no sense. He bent me over that dining table and ignored my half-hearted pleas for him to stop. Deep down, I didn't want him to stop. Everything he did to me felt so good, even the punishment he gave me within minutes of getting me into his home.

Milo breaks the kiss, and I'm panting for air. His ice-blue eyes are blazing with an animalistic need—a need that scares me. My husband is a beast, and he's going to devour me tonight. I can see it in his eyes.

My stomach clenches at the thought. The brief encounters I've had with Milo have been rough. I get the sense that he was holding back on both occasions, which doesn't bode well.

"It's time we departed on our honeymoon," Milo mutters into my ear.

I swallow hard. "Honeymoon?"

He smirks at me. "Of course. It would look a little strange if a man as rich as me didn't sweep his new wife away on a fancy honeymoon, wouldn't it?"

I shake my head. "I don't know. I know nothing about you." It's a sentiment that scares me as I thought I knew everything about this man. He's a cruel and ruthless mob boss who takes whatever he wants, but no one is that black-and-white.

"You don't need to know anything other than the fact that I'm your husband, and you're my property."

I glare at the cocky asshole who still insists I have no rights. "I'll never be your property."

He tilts his head slightly. "Never say never, angel."

He drags me toward the stage where the band is playing. "What are you doing?" I ask, but he ignores me.

Milo grabs the microphone from the stand and taps on it, testing if it's on.

I stand by his side, feeling self-conscious as everyone's attention lands on the two of us. Milo is unpredictable, and I've got no idea what to expect.

"Can I have everyone's attention?" he asks.

The chatter across the room dies down as more attention is directed our way.

"My beautiful bride, Aida, and I would like to thank you for coming. We hope you enjoy the rest of the evening." He tightens his grip on my hand and pulls me closer to him. "However, we have got to be off to catch a plane to our honeymoon destination, which is a closely guarded secret." He winks, and the guests laugh.

It's like I'm witnessing an entirely different man from the one I've met up to now. He's friendly and charismatic when on display, but once we're alone again, his cruel and cold personality will be back in place.

"Thank you all again. Stay as long as you want and drink all night. I would expect nothing less." He waves and everyone claps as he drags me off the stage again.

A beautiful woman with long blonde hair steps into our way. "How cute you two look," she says sarcastically.

Milo tenses next to me and glares at the woman. "Carmella. You have some nerve coming here after what your father pulled at my wedding," he says, his voice quiet but laced with as much threat as if he were shouting.

She laughs, and it isn't kind. "Do I? What are you going to do to me here in front of all these people, Milo?" She sets a hand on the front of his jacket and leans toward him. "Are you going to kill me?" she murmurs hardly loud enough for me to hear.

I clear my throat. "Are you going to introduce me to your friend?"

Carmella takes her hand off my husband. "I'm Carmella, Milo's one and only girlfriend. We broke up a long time ago, though."

Milo grinds his teeth. "Yes, because you slept with one of my friends. What do you want?"

She looks at me for a moment. "Very beautiful, your wife. It would be a shame if she were to end up in an accident."

CRUEL DADDY

Milo growls. I glance around, wondering if this will turn into a scene in front of all these people. "Is that a threat, Carmella?"

She shrugs. "My father doesn't appreciate your lack of respect for me, marrying a woman without consulting me first."

"What are you on about? We broke up almost fifteen years ago. There's no reason for me to consult you."

Her eyes flash with anger. "I know we had our difference, but I always expected that if you were to marry, then you would marry me, and so did my father."

Milo shakes his head. "Then you are both insane. If you would excuse me, we've got a plane to catch." He tries to drag me past his ex, but she steps in my way.

"I'd watch your back if I were you," she says threateningly as I sidestep around her. It's clear she still has feelings for Milo, even if they did split up a long time ago. I find it hard to believe that any woman dated him voluntarily, but perhaps the young Milo was a different man.

Milo leads me out of the ballroom and toward the exit of the house. I yank him to a stop forcefully. "Milo, tell me where exactly we are going?"

He yanks me back, pulling me hard into his chest. "No, princess. It's on a need-to-know basis only, and you don't need to know. All you need to do is shut your mouth and look pretty."

Rage slams into me as I stare at the man my father sold me to. I hate that my father has done this. I will never look at my father the same way again. The fact that he hasn't bothered contacting me since I got here and that I remind him too much of my mother suggests he doesn't want to see me again.

"You're an asshole," I mutter, only loud enough for him to hear.

He growls like a beast and pins me with a gaze that could stop most people's hearts. "It sounds like you want me to punish you, princess."

My stomach twists at the cruel tone of his voice. I shake my head. "No, I want to know where we are going."

He pulls me out of the ballroom and down a quiet corridor, pushing me hard against the wall. Milo's eyes are wild with rage, and I suddenly wonder how much he would hurt me. Does he have control over that rage that so often dances to life in his ice-blue eyes?

"I've tolerated your disobedience up to now, but you are my wife now." He squeezes my throat hard, bringing his face within an inch of mine. "Your sole fucking purpose is to submit to my every order, and if you don't, the punishment will be far worse than what I did to you the first day we met."

There is no lie in his tone. He is deadly serious. It's only now that it finally sinks in how dangerous the man I'm married to is. At times he's addressed me with a flirty tone, but there is nothing but a lethal warning in his voice now.

I bow my head and mutter my reply. "Yes, sir."

He grabs my chin and forces my eyes to meet his gaze. "Now, we're leaving, and you won't ask me where we're going again. Do you understand?"

I nod reluctantly. "Yes, sir."

He searches my gaze for a few more erratic beats of my heart before letting go. "Good. Everything you need is already packed." He grabs my hand hard and yanks me toward the main entrance hall of his home.

I walk with him, trying to keep up. If anyone saw us, they wouldn't think we are a happy newlywed couple, but I don't think Milo cares. James has the limo parked out the front with the engine running, ready to take us wherever we're going.

My heart feels heavy in my chest as I stare at the open door. It's hard to accept that this is my life now. I have no say in anything at all. My father had been controlling and protective, but I always had a sliver of freedom. That small amount of freedom has been torn from me by Milo.

As I stare through the door of the limo, it feels like the door to my dark, cruel future. I've always been a positive person, but I'm struggling to find any positives in my situation.

10

MILO

My jet taxis down the private runway of the airstrip on the outskirts of Boston. It's ten o'clock, and Aida looks tired as she leans back in the leather seat with her eyes shut.

She hasn't got time to be tired as I need to fuck her and take what is mine before we get to the Bahamas. I've rented a private villa on the beach. When we get there, I'll be fucking her so much she won't be able to walk.

She sighs as the plane lifts off the runway. "Are you going to tell me where we are going?" Aida doesn't open her eyes as she speaks.

I push out of my chair and walk behind her. Placing my hands on her shoulders forcefully, I lean over her. "You don't ask me questions, Aida. It seems my first two lessons in discipline didn't sink in. Do I need to be more forceful?"

The tension in her shoulders is satisfying as her eyes flick open and she tries to pull away from me. I hold her firmly in the seat and stop her from escaping.

"I warned you back at my home, but you have to question me." I dig my fingertips into her shoulders hard enough to hurt, leaning over her and forcing her to look up at me over the back of the chair. "Unfortunately for you, I'm never merciful."

The gentle column of her throat bobs as she swallows softly. There's fear in her eyes, and the sight turns me on more than I can explain. As well as the fear, there's an excitement that she can't hide.

"Get up," I say, letting go of her.

This time she does as I say without any smart remarks. A step in the right direction. She stands in front of me, but that fiery defiance is alive in her chestnut brown eyes.

The defiance that I'll enjoy demolishing slowly but surely. "Turn around."

She bites the inside of her cheek before doing as I say. I tease my fingers over the skin at the back of her neck, playing with a curl of her dark, mahogany brown hair.

Aida shudders visibly, even though she's trying hard not to react to my touch. "What are you doing?"

I fumble with the zipper of her dress before roughly pulling it down to reveal her perfect, unblemished skin. It's so strikingly opposite to mine, which is scarred and tattooed. There's not a scar or imperfection on her back, and now it's time to admire every inch. "Drop the dress to the floor," I murmur, taking a step back to watch.

The tension in her shoulders visibly increases as she pulls her dress down and drops it to the floor. Aida steps out of it wearing only white lace matching panties, corset, and garter. I requested that Olivia make sure she wore it without fail under her dress.

The white is a symbol of her pure innocence. Innocence which is about to be infected by darkness so black it could turn the purest of souls rotten. She's an angel, but I'm the devil.

I walk forward and grab her hand, jerking her to face me. "On your knees, angel."

Her eyes widen, searching mine as if trying to work out if I'm serious. "Why?"

I grit my teeth, clenching my jaw. "On your knees," I say more slowly, but infusing my tone with a warning.

She drops to her knees, keeping her gaze on the floor.

I unzip my navy-blue suit pants and free my already rock-hard cock from them. "Look at my cock," I order.

She doesn't move, keeping her eyes on the floor.

I growl at her defiance and grab her chin, forcing her to meet my gaze. "Time for you to taste your husband." I dig my nails into her skin. "Take it."

Her nostrils flare as she holds my gaze before she finally gives in and looks at my cock. The surprise in her eyes is evident as she takes in my size. A few moments tick by, and I feel my patience wearing thin. "I said take it. Don't make me ask again, or you'll regret it."

She closes her fist around the thick girth of my cock and stares up at me, trying hard not to look at it.

"What are you waiting for?" I ask.

She opens her mouth and feebly closes it around my cock. Her reluctance only turns me on as I forcefully grab the back of her head and thrust into the back of her throat.

She gags instantly, placing her hands on my thighs as she tries to push away.

I don't let up, forcing more of my cock down her throat. "You'll take everything I give you when I give it to you," I say, clenching my jaw as the warmth of her mouth drives me wild.

She digs her nails hard into my suit pants, trying to force me away. Saliva spills down her chin and neck as tears prickle her eyes.

Finally, I allow her a moment to breathe. The moment I stop holding her, she pulls away and draws a deep breath. "You bastard. I couldn't breathe."

I grab her forcefully, pulling her to her feet. "Don't call me that ever again, do you understand?" The word grates on my nerves—a word I was called too often growing up because I was born before my parents married.

She nods in response, and I force her back onto her knees.

"Open wide," I order.

Aida opens her jaw wide, and I slip my cock into the back of her throat. She gags instantly, but I don't let up. Every thrust makes saliva spill down her chin as I fuck her mouth. My need to dominate her rules me as I thread my fingers into her dark, thick hair.

Her fingers dig into my thighs as she tries to push me away. It's about time I took away her ability to touch me. As I yank her off my cock, I force her to her feet with her hair. I grab the handcuffs out of the dresser in my jet and dangle them in her face. "Time to make sure you can't fight back, princess."

She shakes her head. "Why are you such an asshole?"

That nickname doesn't anger me as much, but it's still disrespectful. I grab hold of Aida's wrists and force the metal cuffs around her slim, pale wrists. I loosen my tie and force it around her eyes, tying it tightly. "You'll regret speaking to me like that, angel." I bend her over the arm of the chair, gently rubbing my hand over her lace-clad ass.

Aida is still and tense as she remains bent over for me.

I place my foot between her legs and kick them open wide. "Keep your legs wide for me," I say as I grab the waistband of her panties and pull them down. My cock leaks onto the bed at the prospect of tasting her. The word sweet doesn't do her justice. She's more luscious than chocolate.

My mouth salivates as I get on my knees behind her and bury my face in her perfect little pussy.

Aida moans the moment she feels my tongue against her clit, forgetting her mission to prove to me she doesn't enjoy me touching her. Every glare she shoots my way or name she calls me only serves to prove how much she wants me. A woman that didn't want anything from me wouldn't fight the way she does.

"That's it, princess. Moan for daddy," I growl, spanking her flawless ass with the palm of my hand.

She tenses, realizing that she let herself slip up.

I thrust two fingers deep into her tight, virgin pussy, and the tension eases instantly. Her muscles clench my fingers, drawing them deeper. By the time I'm done with my little virgin, she will be a begging, needy whore that answers my every whim and need. It's the only purpose of a wife, and I intend to use her as much as I desire.

I lick her pretty little asshole as I continue to fuck her with my fingers. Once I've thoroughly broken in her tight virgin pussy, then I'll be moving onto her ass. Aida won't know what has hit her. If she thinks I'm an asshole already, I don't know what she will think of me when this honeymoon is over. Quite honestly, I don't care.

We will only be in the Bahamas for a long weekend, but it's enough time to teach her how her life will be from here on in.

As I thrust my fingers into her dripping cunt, I

reach for her hair and pull it. The moan that escapes her voluptuous lips is like music to my ears. The last time I had her in this position, she tried everything possible not to moan. Perhaps keeping away from her for a few days was a good idea, as it seems she can no longer resist me.

"That's it. Moan for me, princess," I growl before devouring her like a predator toying with its prey.

My pure angel doesn't try to fight it anymore. Instead, she submits to the pleasure, moaning with each lap of my tongue and thrust of my fingers.

I stop and have a look in the sideboard in the jet, searching for a flogger. All I've got is a paddle, so I settle on that. It may be rough, but I don't care.

The firm leather will pack a real punch. I return to my wife, who waits obediently. I run the paddle over her skin softly with a light touch before gently tapping her with it.

Aida gasps, shuddering. "What is that—"

I spank her with it harder before she can finish the question. "The more questions you ask, the harsher your punishment will be."

That shuts her up as I slowly drag the paddle across her reddening skin. There is nothing more satisfying than being in control over another person. I paddle her ass two more times, turning it deep red.

Her arousal drips down her thighs as she enjoys the pain. There's no doubt that buried deep inside of this disobedient and fiery little virgin is a submissive soul. I want to uncover that part of her—need to uncover it.

By the time I'm through with her, she'll be a different girl entirely. I'll break her, use her, and then discard her when I'm bored. I paddle her ass twice more on each cheek before burying my face in between her thighs.

Aida moans at the sensation, and I feel her body shudder as she gets closer to orgasm. I will force her to climax repeatedly until she's begging for me to stop.

11

AIDA

I can hardly think straight as Milo teases the tip of his hard cock through the soaking wet entrance of my pussy. My body has a life of its own, denying all the reasoning racing through my mind. I hate this man with a passion, but I crave the way his cruel touch makes me feel.

He's rough and unapologetic—two things I would have thought I'd hate when it comes to such an intimate act. Instead, it turns me on. It's a very strange sensation.

Milo spanks my already red ass, increasing the harsh pain resonating through my flesh. It's unimaginable how pain can turn me on. I'm sure there has to be something fundamentally wrong with me for enjoying this.

The plane dips slightly, reminding me exactly where we are. On a private jet heading to God-knows-where.

It's not exactly the setting I envisaged losing my virginity.

Before my father sold me off to this monster, I had expected to lose my virginity to a man I loved. All my expectations are letting me down lately. It's as though I've gone through life up to now with rose-tinted glasses, and my father tore them from me and smashed them the moment he sold me to Milo.

"Are you ready for daddy's cock?" Milo asks, a coldness to his tone that doesn't match the act we're about to perform.

I shake my head. "Never."

He laughs cruelly behind me, grasping my ass cheeks in his hands. "I do hate liars, angel. I'm pretty sure I told you that before."

Milo nudges the tip of his huge cock at my entrance, making me swallow hard. I clasp my eyes shut, wishing he'd do it and get it over with. It's like ripping off a band-aid—often, the lead-up to it is the worst part.

He bumps the head of his cock against my clit, and the sensation is unparalleled. The pleasure is too much to handle.

I moan, wishing I could stop myself. It's impossible. No matter how much I try to tell myself I hate how this man treats me, I know it's not true. The submissive part of me wants to accept everything he does to me and enjoy it.

"Tell me the truth, princess. Are you ready for

daddy's cock?" he asks again, urging me to speak the words he so badly wants to hear.

Yes, daddy.

My mind repeats those words, but I can't bring myself to say them out loud. The moment I do, I give Milo far too much power, and giving power over your body to a man as dark as Milo is a terrible idea. I may be inexperienced, but I'm not stupid.

"I want to hear you say it," he growls, spanking me with the leather paddle.

I groan at the painful sting that spreads across my ass with each smack of leather. It's strangely arousing, which makes no sense.

He grabs hold of my neck from behind, forcing me to arch my back.

I try to fight against him as he bites my shoulder forcefully, drawing blood. "What are you doing?" I shout, feeling a flood of confusion hit me as my arousal increases.

Milo bites my earlobe. "Punishing a liar."

I grit my teeth together, realizing that there is no way out of this. Milo is relentless. He will keep punishing me until I tell him that I want his cock. It's a notion that should make me sick, but it doesn't. The thought of his cock inside me makes my pussy ache deep within. I long for him in ways I never knew possible.

"Please," I rasp out, needing him to stop his teasing.

I feel his lips curve into a smirk against the skin at the nape of my neck. "Please what?" he asks.

I draw in a deep breath and swallow my pride. "Fuck me," I mumble quietly, feeling defeated inside.

Milo licks a path down the column of my neck. "I didn't quite hear that, angel. Say it louder for daddy."

My pussy aches at his demands. "Fuck me, daddy," I say, letting go of the inhibitions holding me back.

He growls softly before pushing me hard against the leather chair. "That's more like it." The thick tip of his cock teases through my entrance as he drags it through my soaking wet pussy over and over.

I'm ready to explode with need as he continues to play with me like this is just a game. Tears prickle at my eyes as the urgency to be filled with his huge cock intensifies. At that moment, I've never wanted anything more.

"How much do you want daddy's dick?" he asks.

I groan in frustration, trying to fight against the restraints. "For fuck's sake, just give me your cock," I say.

He spanks me hard. "That's not very polite."

I've never felt this frustrated before in my life. "Give me your cock, daddy."

He uses the paddle again on my ass. I'm pretty sure he's bruised me, but I can't seem to find it in me to care. "How badly do you want it?"

"More than anything," I cry out, finally giving in to my sick and twisted desires.

Milo laughs with that same cruel laugh. It grates on my every nerve, but I'm too desperate for release to care. "Good girl," he purrs before thrusting every thick inch of his huge cock deep inside me without warning.

My body bursts into flames. The pain of his huge cock intruding such a tight, untouched part of my body is beyond anything I've ever felt. I can hardly breathe as he starts to move in and out of me, not once asking if I'm okay.

Who the hell am I kidding?

Milo Mazzeo doesn't care about anyone but himself. He would tear me apart and throw me aside once he was done with me without blinking an eye.

His thrusts are rough and hard as he grunts behind me. "Fuck, your tight little virgin cunt is squeezing me like a vice, princess," he growls.

Milo is outrageous with his dirty talk, and it gets my pulse racing. He doesn't care what he says. His confidence is both disgusting and enticing. The handcuffs cut into my soft skin as he uses them to pull me back onto his cock. It feels like he's so deep inside me that there's no other space for him to fill.

I moan as the pain starts to warp into something heavenly. A pleasure of chaotic proportions that threatens to leave me broken. "Oh, God," I cry as his cock drives into me harder and faster with each stroke.

Milo grabs hold of my neck and forces me to arch my back painfully, wrapping his arm around my throat, so I can hardly breathe. "That's it, take daddy's cock and moan like the fucking whore you are."

It feels like I'm no longer in control. All my inhibitions are unbridled. Milo has turned me into a wanton whore, and I don't care. I want him to fuck me so hard that I can't walk straight. It's hard to believe that I've been missing out on a pleasure this tantalizing for over four years since my only chance with Rinaldo.

Deep down, I know that what we would have shared wouldn't have been like this. Rinaldo was a nice guy. He wasn't like Milo, and my body likes the way Milo degrades me.

Milo stills deep inside me, letting go of my throat. His hands move to my hips, and he digs his fingertips in so hard it hurts. "I want to feel that virgin pussy come all over my cock. Do you hear me, Aida?"

I nod my head. "Yes, daddy,"

Milo spanks my ass with the palm of his hand. "Good girl." He slowly moves inside me, hitting the spot that pushes me closer and closer to the edge.

Each impale of his cock is harder and faster, leaving me panting for breath. Milo is a beast—a cruel and unfeeling beast who knows how to make me want him in a way I could never have imagined until tonight.

I can feel my muscles tighten around his thick shaft —a warning that I won't last much longer. "Fuck, daddy, I'm going to come," I cry out as my thighs tremble.

Milo grabs hold of my ass cheeks and parts them

further. "Good. I want to watch that tight pussy come all over my cock," he growls, kneading my ass in his hands. "I want your juice dripping all over me, princess."

My nipples tighten at his words, and I come undone. Every nerve in my body lights on fire as he continues to fuck me through it. He watches as I come all over his huge cock.

"Now it's time for daddy to give you his seed," Milo growls.

I tense at the thought, suddenly realizing that we're fucking without any protection at all. "Wait, don't—"

Milo growls behind me as he explodes inside of me. I feel his cum shooting deep inside of my pussy as he thrusts again and again, draining every drop. My body remains tense as panic starts to rise inside of me. There's no way I want to get pregnant with this monster's baby.

Once he's finished, he pulls out.

I straighten up and turn to glare at him as he tucks his cock back into his suit pants. "I'm not on the pill or anything, so that was a dumb move."

There's amusement dancing in his ice-blue eyes as he meets my gaze. "You're my wife now, Aida. I expect you to provide me an heir. I'm going to keep breeding you until you produce what I want."

I stare at him in shock. He never mentioned having his child, but I guess it is a natural progression—marriage then kids.

He walks to the other end of the plane and draws a curtain between us. I've never felt so used in all my life as I feel the cum drip from my abused pussy.

Milo is the monster I expected. I can't understand why his coldness hurts so badly when I always expected it. I think it's because he just took such an intimate thing from me. Milo took it as though it meant nothing. A right he has as my husband.

I grit my teeth, knowing I hate him more than ever. I hate him and I want him, two things that should never co-exist. This honeymoon is going to be hell, and it's hardly even started yet.

12

MILO

The villa on the beach is secluded and perfect for the antics I have planned with my new wife. The island has hardly any residents, which means we won't see many other people. I stare out of the floor-to-ceiling windows at my wife walking along the white sand beach.

Aida strolls toward the sea. I watch her as she dips her toes in. It's the early morning here in the Bahamas, and the sun is painting the sky in a mix of orange and yellow.

Aida thought I was asleep when she snuck out of the bedroom, dressing silently. It's amusing how clueless she can be. I'm her master now. Everything she does, I will know. My life doesn't lend to having a wife who can do whatever the fuck she wants. It'll take time for her to accept my position of dominance over her in day-to-day life, but she will accept it.

I sip my coffee, watching her like a hawk. Aida is entirely unaware that she's being watched as she throws her hands above her head and twirls around in the surf.

I can't help but feel in awe of her unbreakable positivity, even in the circumstances she's found herself in. There's something beautiful about her strength, but I've seen women like her break in the end. I know that I will tire of her in time, but surprisingly, after our first night together, I want her more.

I knock back the rest of my coffee before opening the sliding door out onto the wrap-around porch. A warm breeze embraces me the moment I step outside into the humid Caribbean air. It's been a long time since I took a break away from the city, but people would have questioned my relationship with Aida if we didn't go on a honeymoon, especially with my wealth.

I walk down the porch steps and silently move toward Aida, who is unaware of my presence. She looks in her element on the beach, but I guess this is the kind of setting she is used to. After all, Aida grew up on an island in the Mediterranean.

My cock throbs in my swim shorts as I make my way toward her. All she's wearing is a bikini and sheer beach dress that I asked Olivia to pack. Aida hasn't been allowed to keep many of her clothes, so I had Olivia pick out her new wardrobe with one instruction—make sure everything she buys is sexy.

Once I'm about a meter behind Aida, I clear my throat.

Her shoulders stiffen, and she turns around slowly. When our eyes meet, that raw electricity pulses between us. No matter how much she tries to deny it, the sexual attraction is undeniable.

"What are you doing out here?" she asks, folding her arms over her chest.

I tilt my head to the side. "Are you asking what I'm doing on the private beach of the villa I rented?" The girl has real tenacity, considering her position in this relationship.

She shakes her head. "No, but you can't sneak up on people like that."

I smirk at her. "Bad choice of word."

Her lip quivers and she turns away from me to look across the expansive ocean again.

I feel my blood boil at the fact that she dares to tell me I can't do something and then turns her back on me as if I'm unimportant.

Aida must love punishment. Otherwise, she would have learned by now that making me angry only results in pain for her. I grab her by the hips, and she gasps, turning rigid the moment my hands are on her. "Never turn your back on me again, do you understand?" I growl.

Aida nods her head slowly. "Yes, sir," she says, condescension lacing her tone.

I let it slide. "Face me, angel." I love calling her an angel because that's what she is. A pure and innocent angel who has fallen into the hands of the devil.

She turns around and glares at me. My savage deflowering hasn't broken her spirit, which means she's strong. A lot of women would have been broken by it.

I hate the admiration I feel pooling in my stomach. It's not something I'm used to feeling for anyone. "Give your husband a good morning kiss," I order.

The fire in her beautiful, deep brown eyes makes me harder than nails. Aida's about five foot seven, which isn't short. However, I am almost a foot taller than her at six foot six. She tries to reach me by stretching onto her tiptoes, but she's not tall enough.

I smirk and then lower my head, bringing my lips to hers. Our lips meet as Aida tries to pull away after a brief touch, but my hard, throbbing cock has other ideas.

I forcefully grab her hips and hold her against me. My tongue drives past her lips and devours her mouth. It's the first kiss we've shared since we got here.

Aida watched me walk away from her after claiming her virginity with sadness in her eyes. I watched on the CCTV in the jet as she curled up in the armchair, and tears flooded down her cheeks. It was a strangely beautiful scene to watch.

When we got to the villa, she went straight to bed and was asleep by the time I joined her. My fear that I'd broken her resolve on the plane was unfounded, since here she is with that feisty fire burning in her eyes. I like her fighting me. It makes it more enjoyable.

Aida pushes me away, breaking the kiss. "You're the most frustrating man I've ever met."

I tilt my head slightly and smile at her. "Good, I'm glad I've gotten under your skin."

She shakes her head and groans, turning her back on me for the second time and walking away.

My jaw clenches. "Aida, what did I tell you?"

She glances over her shoulder, and there's a devious glint in her eyes. Suddenly, she starts into a sprint into the sea and then dives in, swimming away from me.

I growl as my prey tries to escape me, diving in after her.

Aida is a good swimmer, stronger than I expected as she makes good ground in front of me, but I'm faster. In the end, I manage to catch her about twenty meters along the shore.

She squeals as my arms wrap tightly around her waist.

I pull her back flush against my chest. "I warned you not to turn your back on me, and swimming away from me is even worse," I murmur into her ear, letting her feel the hard press of my cock against her skimpily clad body.

Aida didn't bother removing the sheer beach dress before plunging headfirst into the warm sea. "Sorry, sir," she says, her voice laced with desire.

I think my rough handling of her last night backfired. Normally, the women I pay to fuck don't enjoy the pain I dole out, but Aida does. It's a dilemma that will become difficult to handle. Granted, I was tame with her on the plane because I didn't have a full range of equipment. Aida loved it, though.

"You'll have to pay for your disobedience, but first, we have a schedule to maintain." I bite her earlobe hard enough to hurt. "A schedule that your escapade is going to make keeping difficult. We're already late."

Aida glances at me over her shoulder. "Maybe we should scrap the schedule then." She pushes her ass harder into my cock.

It takes all my willpower to resist, but I won't give in to her devious seduction. One fuck, and she's transformed from an innocent angel to a seductive hellion. "No. Now come inside and get ready," I order.

Aida's shoulders drop in disappointment. It's hard to believe after the rough fuck I gave her last night and my swift exit that she is in any state for more. I expected her to be too sore to fuck today but intended to fuck her anyway. What I didn't expect was for her to want it. "Fine," she huffs, releasing herself from my hold and swimming to the shore.

I watch her and can't help but smile. Aida surprises me every chance she can, and I know that's dangerous. She's unpredictable. I don't do unpredictable, but the thought of not having her at my mercy is unappealing. Aida has become intriguing to me. Until I figure her out, I won't be able to get her out of my system.

The warm water washes around me as the waves crash into the shore. All the beauty of this island pales compared to the woman walking across the beach. Every step she takes makes her hips sway delectably.

I'm irritated that I made plans, but Anita is booked to take us on an island tour. Our honeymoon pictures need to be convincing when we show them to the mayor. After our first impression of him as a couple, I'm not sure we were that convincing.

The last thing I need is for Thomas to stop backing me in my endeavors to take more power in Boston. My bid to get onto the city council has been in play for over three years, and my wife won't take that away from me.

A charity gala is due to be held the night we return to Boston, and we will be there playing the convincing role of newlyweds. I've got a lot of work to do when it comes to Aida, but three more days on this island could help with that.

I dive into the water and swim to the shore, knowing we don't have long until Anita shows up at the door. My wife's antics mean I need to shower, dry, and dress again.

She will need to be punished for it, but that can wait until tonight. Today, we will act like a normal, happy couple on honeymoon.

13

AIDA

"Hello, I'm Anita, and I'll be doing your island tour," the lady standing at the front door says.

My brow furrows. "Island tour?"

She smiles, holding her hand to her chest. "Oh, was it a surprise?" She shakes her head, glancing behind me. "I'm so sorry, Mr. Mazzeo. I didn't realize."

My body tenses when I realize he's behind me. The predator that popped my cherry on the plane and walked away as if taking my virginity meant nothing.

"Not to worry, Anita. She had to find out at some point." He wraps his arms tightly around my waist, kissing my neck. "I thought you'd enjoy a tour of the island today." There's an alarmingly affectionate tone to his voice rather than the usual coldness.

I nod. "That sounds lovely."

My heart skips a beat as he entwines his fingers with mine. "Let's go, then. Is the boat out front?"

"Yes, it's ready on the dock." Anita looks at us and smiles. "What a beautiful couple you two make." She winks at Milo. "You'll have beautiful children."

My stomach churns as I remember Milo's reaction when I told him I wasn't on the pill.

I'm going to keep breeding you until you produce what I want.

A shudder races down my spine. I'm nothing more to this man than a prize bitch to impregnant and discard when he's done with me. It's a chilling notion but a dismally true one.

I hate him more than ever after the way he took my virginity. My expectations met reality, but I'd hoped I was somehow wrong about Milo Mazzeo. The sickest part is that I wanted him again this morning when I felt his hard length pressed against my ass. My mind hates him, but my body craves his touch. Desire is more complicated than I could have imagined.

Milo guides me out the back of the villa and down the sandy beach toward the dock where a small yacht waits for us. Anita follows behind us as Milo keeps his hand tight around mine. It feels like he's changed his entire personality suddenly as he helps me onto the boat.

"Wow, this is lovely," I say, noticing the hot tub on the deck and the large sun bed next to it.

Milo wraps an arm around my back. "Sit back and enjoy it, angel," he murmurs into my ear. "This is going to be the most fun you'll have on this trip." That cold, cruel tone returns, and my stomach sinks like a lead weight.

Anita claps her hands. "Right, so first stop will be Compass Cay Marina to swim with the nurse sharks."

I tense at that, wondering if she's serious. Swimming with sharks is not on my bucket list.

Milo smirks. "Don't tell me you are scared of sharks, angel?"

I glare at him and don't answer. I'm not admitting any of my fears to him. If I do, he will probably throw me overboard with them. I sit on the large day bed and dangle my toes into the hot tub in the center.

Anita smiles. "It's about a twenty-minute journey from here, so sit back and relax." She walks toward a small bar set up to one side. "Can I get you two love birds something to drink?"

"Whiskey on the rocks," Milo answers.

I stare at him with wide eyes. "It's barely ten in the morning."

He shrugs. "We're on holiday."

Anita pours the drink. "And for you?"

"I'll have an orange juice, please."

She smiles and pours my more sensible drink for the morning before bringing them over. "Is there anything else I can get you?" Anita asks.

Milo shakes his head. "No, that's all. Thank you, Anita."

Anita nods. "I'll leave the both of you in peace then."

I watch as she walks toward the front of the boat and disappears. A snap of a camera draws my attention back to my husband. Milo has a camera around his neck and takes a few photos of the boat and the view. "I didn't know you were into photography."

He looks at me and laughs. "I'm not, but when we attend the charity event next week with a lot of the guests at our reception, they're going to expect to see photos." He raises a brow. "We need to make this convincing."

I shake my head and pull my beach dress off, revealing the overly revealing swimsuit that Olivia packed for me. Luckily, it has a full bottom area of fabric covering the bruises Milo gave me on the airplane. It's red with hardly any fabric to cover my breasts but holds them together perfectly.

Milo's gaze pins to me as I stand and walk down the steps into the warm water of the hot tub. He's no longer taking photos. Instead, he's watching me with a predatory gaze—a gaze that makes me feel unusually powerful. The fact that a man as cold as him can be distracted by my body so easily is empowering.

I could sense his surprise when I tried to seduce him in the sea. He expected me to be a broken shell of a woman after the way he fucked me and left me. I won't let him break me already. If I let Milo have the upper hand, then I know I won't survive him.

Milo pulls his shirt off and sets the camera on top of it before joining me in the tub. "Did I give you permission to get into the tub?" he asks, wrapping a strong, tattooed arm around my waist and pulling my back against him.

I shake my head. "You said to sit back and enjoy it while I can." I shrug. "That's what I'm doing."

His warm breath teases against the nape of my neck as he plants a soft kiss there. A kiss that is so opposite to the way he has kissed me any other time. There's nothing soft or gentle about Milo. "Now, smile and look pretty," he murmurs as he reaches for the camera on the day bed.

I grit my teeth, knowing it's almost impossible to smile in my situation.

"I said smile, angel." He grazes his teeth gently across the back of my neck, tickling me.

I smile involuntarily, and he snaps the photo. He checks it on the screen, and it's a ridiculous sight. If someone didn't know the truth about our arranged marriage and my hatred for this man, we would look like a normal couple on honeymoon. It's an image that couldn't be further from the truth and drives home the old-time saying, "don't judge a book by its cover."

"You look beautiful," Milo says with an alarming sincerity in his deep baritone voice. "A real angel."

I look at the photo. "An angel caught by the devil himself," I murmur.

Anita clears her throat behind us. "We're pulling

into Compass Cay. Are you two ready for an experience of a lifetime?"

Milo nods and squeezes me. "We sure are. Don't worry, Aida. I'll protect you." His act falls into place whenever Anita is around, and it makes my skin crawl. Protect me. He'll do the opposite to me. Bend me, break me, and discard me when he's had enough.

He exits the hot tub before turning around and offering me his hand.

I meet his ice-blue gaze, and my heart somersaults at the fiery desire burning in them. His normally cold and impossible-to-read expression entirely melted away. I wonder if that's part of his act.

"What are you waiting for, angel?"

I place my hand tentatively in his and allow him to help me out of the hot tub—not that I needed the help. His new chivalrous ways are weird. We walk toward the back of the boat to disembark onto the dock. My stomach drops when I gaze into the water surrounding the boat and see sharks swimming beneath the surface.

"Isn't it dangerous to swim with sharks?"

Anita shrugs. "They can bite at times if you're not careful. You don't have to swim with them if you don't want."

Milo squeezes my hand. "What's life without a bit of danger?"

I shake my head. "I think I'll sit this one out."

Milo squeezes my hand so hard in warning it hurts, but I know he can't force me.

"No problem, Aida, you can watch Milo." Anita signals at his camera. "You can be the photographer instead."

Milo looks angry as I reach for the camera in his other hand. "I wanted to experience this together, Aida." There's a threat in his tone that to most people's ears wouldn't be detectable.

I met Milo less than a week ago, but he has threatened me enough times for me to know. I set my hand on his muscular arm plastered with tattoos and meet his gaze. "I'm sorry, honey, this is something I can't do." The use of that word seems to enrage him more, but we're supposed to be acting like a normal newlywed couple.

Milo passes the camera into my hand, lingering a moment. He finally walks away and joins the insane people getting into the water with the sharks. I notice a sign warning that occasionally, the sharks can bite and that you swim at your own risk. There's no way Milo is getting me in that water.

I watch as my husband walks down the steps fearlessly. Most of the tourists here are getting into the water. Until this morning, I hadn't seen Milo this naked as he's wearing just a pair of swim shorts. The tattoos on his chest and arms give him a rougher appearance, as well as several nasty-looking scars. Even when he took my virginity on the plane last night, he was dressed, with only his cock through the zipper.

Anita approaches and leans on the railing, watching Milo. "How are you doing, sweetie?"

I shrug, wishing I could talk to someone about Milo and this sham of an arranged marriage.

Milo blocked my friend's mobile numbers on my cell phone after he caught me talking to them. Besides sending messages on social media, which thankfully he hasn't blocked, I've got no way of talking to them properly. I sigh. "I'm doing good. It's so beautiful here."

Anita nods. "Indeed. I'm blessed that this is my home." Her brow furrows slightly. "From your accent, it sounds like you didn't grow up in America?"

I shake my head. "No, I was born and raised in Sicily."

"Ah, so you moved to marry Mr. Mazzeo?" she asks.

I nod, feeling a sadness pulling at my chest. "Yes. I miss the island life very much. Boston isn't exactly special like the Bahamas or Sicily."

"No, but if the man you love is in Boston, then that's where your heart is."

I swallow hard and nod in response, wishing that were true. Milo isn't the man I love. He's the man I hate. A vindictive man who believes a wife is for nothing more than breeding. It's archaic and barbaric.

Milo waves at me from the sea to get my attention as a shark swims past him.

I bring the camera up and take a photo, which is surprisingly good. It's odd watching Milo smile and enjoy himself, but I wonder if it's all an act for the camera. Milo has a stunning smile when he's not smirking at me cruelly, but I've only seen it here on this island.

Milo swims for a short while before returning to the jetty and joining me. He places a hand on either side of me on the rails, closing me in so I can't escape him. "You missed an exhilarating swim," he murmurs into my ear.

I shrug. "I don't like sharks."

Milo forces me to turn around and face him. "They're just misunderstood." There's something in his tone, as if he's talking about himself.

"What's next on the itinerary?" I ask.

He smirks at me. "Not sure you can handle it, but we're going to go and swim with the pigs."

I stare at him in confusion, wondering if that's a euphemism for something. "Swim with the pigs?"

He nods. "Yes, you'll see when we get there." Milo signals over Anita. "Can we head on over to Big Major Cay now?"

She nods. "Sure, hop aboard, and we'll get going." Her attention moves to me, and she smiles. "I'm sure you'll be fine swimming with the pigs."

Milo leads me back onto the deck of the yacht and sits down.

"Why would pigs be in the sea or swimming?"

He laughs, but it's not that cruel laugh I usually hear. It's easy and almost friendly. "No one knows why they are on the beach and why they swim there." Milo wraps an arm around me and pulls me against him. "Some people believe they must have been on a ship that got wrecked, whereas others believe pirates owned them for food but never returned. It's a mystery."

I smile at the thought of pigs swimming. "It sounds like fun."

Milo's lips tease against my neck, and he kisses me there again. "It does," he says quietly.

An easy silence falls between us as I allow Milo to hold me against him. It's unusual how comfortable I feel in the arms of a beast.

After another thirty minutes of cruising through the ocean, the boat slows. Milo points to something in the sea. "There they are, coming to greet us."

I blink a couple of times to work out if what I'm seeing is real. Pigs are swimming to the boat in the shallow water as we come to a stop about twenty meters from the shore.

Anita joins us on the deck. "There's no port here, so you'll have to disembark directly into the water or the rowboat if you're not a strong swimmer."

"I'm a strong swimmer. This is so exciting." I walk enthusiastically to the steps which lead down into the sea below. The pigs are quite a few meters up ahead in the shallow water.

Milo grabs my hand. "Let's jump in together."

I pout at him. "If I jump in, I'll mess up my hair."

He laughs. "Don't be such a pussy." He holds my hand tightly. "On three. One. Two. Three." We both jump into the cool water, which is a relief from the humid heat.

Milo grabs me by the waist as we swim up to the surface. He kisses me the moment we come up for air, and it takes me by surprise until I see Anita taking photos of us. He planned the photo.

"Come on, let's go and see those pigs," he says, swimming away from me.

I follow him but feel uneasy about the disappointment rising inside of me. He planned the kiss and this entire day. His actions are all an act. I need to keep reminding myself of that before I fall into a trap far more deadly than the one which I'm already entangled in.

14

MILO

As the day draws to a close, the boat pulls up at our private dock. The beach has been prepared with a dining table so we can have dinner together and watch the sunset.

It's a romantic setting that doesn't sit well with me. Although I know that our photo album wouldn't be complete without a romantic dinner, I'd rather be punishing my wife for her constant disobedience throughout the day.

Anita is standing by the steps to disembark the boat.

"Thank you for a wonderful tour, Anita."

She smiles widely. "Of course. If you want to charter the boat again during your stay, then you have my number. I hope you both have a wonderful evening." There's a glint of amusement in her eyes, as she knows what a typical honeymoon evening will consist of. What she doesn't know is how dark and twisted my tastes are.

"Thanks, but I think we are just going to take it easy for the rest of our stay."

Anita nods. "Look me up when you're next back in The Exumas."

"Will do. Thank you again." I give her a wave and then grab Aida's hip, pulling her into my side. "I should be taking you straight into the house and punishing you," I growl into her ear.

She tenses, shivering. "But you're not going to?"

I shake my head and point at the dining table. "No, because we're going to watch the sunset over dinner. But then I'm going to punish you for your disobedience today."

Her eyes flash with irritation, but there's a hint of excitement too. Aida wants me to punish her. I feel my cock hardening in my pants at the thought. Her ass will be bruised today, and yet she wants more.

I clear my throat, breaking the overwhelming sexual tension between us. "The food will be getting cold, and it's almost time for the sunset." I grab hold of my camera and hold it up. "We need to make sure we get some convincing romantic photos."

Aida looks disappointed as she bows her head. "Yes, sir." She walks by my side toward the small table, which is lit by candles. The waitress who comes with the villa is standing dutifully to one side.

Once we are seated, she approaches. "What can I get you both to drink?"

I meet Aida's gaze, which is conflicted as she looks at me. "Surely you will have an alcoholic drink tonight?" I raise a brow, remembering her comment when I asked for a whiskey at ten o'clock in the morning.

She looks at the waitress. "I'll have a glass of prosecco."

"Not champagne?" I ask.

Aida shakes her head. "I prefer prosecco. After all, I'm Italian."

I smile at her, admiring the way she sticks to her heritage. "Fair enough. A bottle of your finest prosecco it is."

Amelia, the waitress, bows her head. "I'll bring it right away." She grabs two small cocktail glasses and places one in front of each of us. "While you wait, this is a rum punch, a popular Bahamian drink."

"Thank you," Aida says, bringing it up to her lips and tasting a sip. "Wow, that is strong," she says, eyes wide.

Amelia nods. "It's got a lot of rum in it, so take it steady." The waitress disappears toward the house to retrieve the prosecco. It dawns on me at that moment that I hardly know anything about my new wife.

I don't know what her favorite drink is or her favorite food. If we were being quizzed about each other, we'd fail for sure. It's not in my nature to want to know anything about another person, but still I say, "Tell me three facts about you, Aida."

Aida looks up from her drink with her brow furrowed. "What?"

I clench my jaw. "I said, tell me three facts about you." I scrub a hand across the back of my neck. "How are we supposed to be a convincing couple in public if we know nothing about each other?"

She sucks on the straw in her glass innocently, but it's a sight that has me hard in seconds. "I don't know, not talk to anyone?"

"While I do like that option, I would like to know three facts about you."

Her brow furrows as she thinks. "What do you want to know?"

"Tell me what your favorite food is."

"Easy. Pasta," she replies without hesitating.

"What about your favorite color?" I ask, watching as she plays with a strand of her dark brown hair nervously.

"Teal blue, like the sea in Sicily."

I rub a hand over my beard, which feels rough and messy from swimming in the sea. "Your favorite place?"

"Palermo for sure."

My brow furrows. "My father was from Sicily." I meet her inquisitive chestnut gaze. "What do you miss most about Sicily?"

Aida thinks about this question more carefully, and

there's a sadness in her eyes. "My friends. I miss my friends the most."

It's an odd notion to me. All my life, I've made sure I depend on no one. Friends are a weakness that a don of a mafia can't indulge in. The closest thing I have to a friend is Piero, and even he fears me. It's the way my father brought me up.

Aida tilts her head. "What about you?"

"What about me?"

She sighs. "What are your answers to the questions?"

I narrow my eyes at her. "My favorite food is pizza, my favorite color is grey, and my favorite place is Cape Cod. I used to go there as a kid with my mother."

Aida looks intrigued at the mention of family. "Where is your mother now?"

I clench my jaw. "Dead."

Her gaze turns wistful, and she nods. "So is mine."

I'm glad she doesn't apologize because she's dead, since it's a sentiment I never understood. Instead, she has the same experience as me, and that is far more powerful. "How old were you when your mother died?" I ask.

Aida's eyes sparkle with unshed tears. "Eleven years old. You?"

I feel a knot in my throat as I think back to the day she died. It was my fault. My mother always told me not to play in my father's office, no matter what. That day, she left me alone for a while, and like a dumb kid, I went into his office and broke a priceless vase.

When he returned and my mother told him, the frenzy he broke into was unprecedented. He beat her harder than he'd ever beaten her before while I crouched down behind the sofa. She died of her injuries a day later after being rushed into hospital. She had too much internal bleeding.

"I was seven years old," I reply, feeling a small amount of weight lift from my shoulders at telling someone. Ever since my mother's death, I've not spoken about her to anyone.

Aida twirls her hair around her finger. "That must have been hard. I thought I was young."

I'm not sure why I told Aida about my mother. Perhaps it's because if she is to be my wife, she needs to know the intimate details of my family's past. "That's enough heavy talk on our honeymoon," I say, desperate to change the subject. "Tell me about Sicily."

Amelia finally returns with our prosecco and our first course. The entire meal is vegetarian for Aida, as I don't care too much what I eat. A small Bahamian salad is the first course.

I can't help but watch my wife as she savors every bite of the delicious black bean salad. It's refreshing after a hot day out in the sun. "How is it?"

She stops mid-bite and blushes. "It's delicious. Sorry, I get so focused when I'm eating, I forget to talk."

I laugh. Today I've laughed more than I have in too many years to count. "No need to apologize for that."

She sips her prosecco, taking a break from the food. "It's delicious, thank you." I'm surprised by the sincerity in her tone. The defensive walls she erects around her have disappeared tonight.

Her eyes widen as all her attention is drawn to the sun setting behind the horizon. The reason for the dinner in the first place. I grab my camera and take a couple of photos before standing and taking one of Aida watching the sunset.

"That's so beautiful," she says.

I nod, staring at the woman in front of me. "It is indeed."

Aida's attention moves to me, and she flushes when she realizes I was staring at her instead of the sunset. I've seen enough sunsets in my lifetime.

I return to my seat and the evening goes more smoothly than I imagined. We eat and drink, talking about trivial things such as our favorite music and movies. I haven't spoken to someone so easily in a long time.

As it gets later, I only have one thing on my mind. Aida holds my gaze as all my thoughts slide into the gutter. My cock is as hard as a rock in my tight pants, which I changed into on the yacht. We showered and got ready for dinner on route back to the villa.

I stand from my seat and walk slowly around the

back of Aida's, setting my hands on her tense shoulders. "Stand up."

She obeys me without hesitation.

I grab hold of her hips and bend her over the table we'd been eating at. "It's time for me to punish you, angel."

"Milo," she gasps my name in surprise. "What about the waitress?"

"Fuck the waitress," I growl, spanking her ass.

"Ouch," she cries, trying to escape from me. "I'm too sore—"

I grab her throat, forcing her to arch her back. "Maybe you should have thought about that when you disobeyed me today."

She whimpers and not in a good way.

I can't understand why regret creeps into the back of my mind. We were having a nice dinner. I would go so far as to say we were enjoying each other's company until I lost my shit and decided to bend Aida over the table. It's what I do. I don't know how to act differently with a woman.

I lift the hem of her dress, and my cock jumps in my tight boxer briefs at the sight of her bruised ass cheeks. I made my mark on her last night, which turns me on.

I gently run my hand across her ass, making her shiver. "Do these hurt?" I ask, gently pressing one of the bruises. I don't sleep with the same woman twice, so I never see the aftermath despite knowing I'm heavy-handed with my implements.

CRUEL DADDY

Aida shrugs, glancing over her shoulder at me. "They're sore."

I rub my hand softly over the curve of her ass, making her shiver. Instead of spanking Aida, I continue to caress her sore skin. "Don't worry, angel. I won't spank you again tonight, but I am going to fuck you so hard you can't walk straight." I pull her by her hair, forcing her upright. "We're alone now. The waitress left after dessert."

Aida moans as I push aside her panties and slide my fingers between the slick lips of her pussy, groaning when I feel how wet she is.

"You've been sitting here all night gagging for my cock, haven't you?" I ask, thrusting a finger deep inside her tight pussy.

She moans, nodding. "Yes, daddy."

Her instant submission makes my cock jump. Last night she held on and fought her needs, but now she's ready to beg me for it. "You're such a dirty little whore, Aida. My dirty little whore." I yank her hair, clenching my teeth as I know I can't spank her no matter how badly I want to.

It takes all my self-control not to hurt her the way a broken part of me wants to. Instead, I let go of Aida's hair and spin her around to face me. There's a mix of anticipation and anxiety in her eyes as she waits for me to make the next move. I kiss her passionately, taking out my frustrations on her mouth as my tongue plunders it.

Her hands roam over my shoulders as she touches me for the first time. It's a foreign sensation, being touched. Aida slides her hand under my shirt, tensing when her fingers tease over the scar on my chest.

I've never let any woman I've been with touch me. I can't understand why I'm letting Aida. She pushes my shirt over my head, and I allow her. Her first time with anyone, I kept my clothes on and made it anything but special for her. Perhaps I can correct some of the wrongs tonight.

Why the hell do I even want to?

Aida moans into my mouth as I grip her hips tightly and pull her closer. The conflict inside of me widens as my need to dominate her overrules me. "On your hands and knees," I order.

She drops to the floor without hesitating, looking up at me with dilated eyes.

I loosen the button on my shorts and drop them to the floor, stepping out of them. Then, I lose my boxer briefs.

Aida waits patiently, licking her lips at the sight of my cock. It drives me wild to see her so hungry for me. The innocent princess who has fought to resist the palpable attraction between us. All that fight is gone now she's had a taste.

"Suck it, angel," I order.

She grabs hold of me and brings her pouty, full lips to the tip.

I groan as she closes her mouth around me, sucking

at the tip as her tongue swirls in circles. "Fuck, your mouth feels like heaven," I grunt, allowing her the freedom to take control, only for a moment, and then I grab a fistful of her hair forcefully and thrust my cock deep into her throat.

She gags, digging her fingertips into my thighs as she tries to push me away. I don't let her. No matter how much I should make up for my roughness with her on that plane when I took her virginity, this is who I am. A dark and twisted beast that does not know how to be gentle.

Aida gasps for air when I finally stop fucking her throat. "You're going to kill me," she says, tears prickling at her eyes from the force. She holds her throat, staring at me in shock.

I shake my head. "No, princess, I know what I'm doing." I grab her chin and search her eyes. "You need to relax and trust me."

A whisper of disbelief enters her expression. "Trust you?" She shakes her head. "You haven't given me any reason to trust you."

I smirk at that. "I've given you the best orgasm you've ever had. Open your mouth," I order.

She hesitates for a moment before slowly opening her mouth.

I spit into it, and surprisingly she moans. "You're mine, and you do as I say, angel. So, if I tell you to trust me, you trust me." I kiss her tempting mouth, letting my tongue delve inside desperately.

My innocent angel is slowly turning into my dirty little whore. I love how easy she is to bend to my will. She'll be eating out of the palm of my hand on command by the time we leave the Bahamas.

"Now, I want you to take your panties off for me and bend over again."

She does as I say, bending over the table and glancing at me over her shoulder as she drags her panties down.

I groan at the sight of her wet pussy nestled between her creamy thighs. My cock pulses, desperate to be buried deep inside of my wife. I could never have imagined how much I'd want the woman I'd agreed to marry without ever meeting her.

I fist my aching cock in my hands before bringing the tip to her entrance.

Aida quivers, her thighs shaking with anticipation.

The power I feel being able to take whatever the fuck I want from her is exhilarating.

Slowly, I drag the tip of my cock through her dripping pussy. Aida moans, and I feel that sound right to my balls.

"Tell me how much you want to feel daddy's cock breeding that naughty little cunt."

She gasps softly, arching her back. "I want your cock so bad, daddy," she says, her voice whiny and perfect. "Please give it to me."

I run my finger over her perfect, tight asshole, a hole I'd love to fuck, but for now, her tight, barely used pussy will do. I'm going to breed her until my cum is dripping down her thighs. Until she's so full, she can't take anymore. I want Aida growing big and round with my baby as the ultimate proof that I own her. I own my dirty, little whore who tried to fight against this primal instinct we're both driven by.

I don't tease her any longer, burying every inch of my cock deep inside of her with one stroke.

She's so wet tonight that I slide inside her easily.

Her muscles clamp around me as she moans loudly into the night air.

She doesn't care who might hear. She doesn't care that she's proving to me how much she craves me. It's sexy as hell.

"That's it, angel, take daddy's cock inside of you," I murmur, digging my fingertips hard into her hips.

Aida arches her back more. The dark bruises on her butt cheeks only turn me on more. It's my mark on her body. The marks I left when I took her virginity.

"Who owns you?" I ask, thrusting in and out of her hard and slow.

She groans before answering me. "You do, daddy," she says in a sing-song voice that sets my nerves on fire.

"That's right," I growl, feeling that angry need to dominate rise to the surface. "I own all of you, Aida. I own this perfect little cunt. I own your tight, perfect body. You're my slave and my whore. I'll fuck you when I want, and you will fucking like it." I wrap a hand around her throat from behind, forcing her to arch her back even more. "By the time the night is through, your body will be full of my seed. I won't rest until I've bred you," I purr into her ear.

Aida's moans are wanton now as she almost cries with pleasure. "Yes, fuck, yes. Breed me, daddy."

I bite her shoulder hard, keeping hold of her throat as I pound into her with all my strength. Never have I been so desperate for a woman. "I need you to milk my cock with your tight little pussy. I need you to come for daddy."

"Fuck," she cries as she tumbles over the edge. Her muscles clamp hard around my throbbing cock.

It's impossible not to explode inside of her. I growl as my release hits me. My cock pulses deep inside of her, filling her with my seed. I've never had such a primitive instinct to fuck a woman before in my life.

Aida turns limp as I continue to hold her throat more softly now. She's panting for air, and so am I. Both of us remain silent for a long while, with my cock still buried deep inside of her.

Aida jiggles slightly, and it's enough to stir the need in my balls again. My cock twitches inside of her, making her gasp.

"Don't relax yet, angel. We've barely even started."

15

AIDA

I sit on the sand with my feet in the surf, listening to the soothing sound of the ocean. Three days here have flown by faster than I expected, and we're due to leave tonight for Boston.

I've had some time alone on the trip while Milo talks on the phone to his men or works on deals that he won't discuss in front of me. Our marriage has started better than I expected, but I know that's because we're here in the Bahamas. Once we're back in Boston, the cruel man I first met will return with vigor.

It's why I don't want to leave this island. Not to mention, Boston is so depressing in comparison to the Bahamas or Sicily. I'm used to living by the sea.

I think there's something wrong with me for liking the rough way Milo handles me. Although, I wish he would hold me afterwards. He keeps a distance between us, and for some reason, that hurts.

"Morning, angel," Milo says from behind me, making me jump.

I hate the way my stomach somersaults and my pulse races the moment I hear his voice. This trip was a mistake since my passionate hatred for this man has twisted into a passionate need for him.

"Good morning, sir," I reply, knowing he likes me to call him that.

He sits down in the sand and puts his legs on either side of me, kissing the nape of my neck in a way that makes me melt between my thighs.

I moan as his teeth tease at my shoulder. "What time are we leaving?"

Milo bites my neck softly. "A car is picking us up in four hours. We have time to enjoy the island a bit longer together," he murmurs.

An ache ignites in my chest the moment he says that word: together. My feelings toward Milo are getting complicated. I've heard that giving away your virginity can bond you to the man that takes it, but everything Milo has done should have made that impossible.

"What do you have in mind?" I ask.

Milo stands up and walks in front of me, holding out a hand. "Let me show you."

I close my hand around his and allow him to pull me to my feet.

Milo grabs my beach dress and pulls it over my head, tossing it to one side. "We're going for a swim."

I swallow hard as he leads me into the sea before

letting go of my hand and swimming toward the left of the cove.

My brow furrows as I watch for a moment before following him into the water. I've always loved swimming and used to be on the swim team at school in Sicily. It's one of the most freeing experiences and better in the ocean. However, I can't deny that those sharks we saw at Compass Cay Marina shook me up. There are no sharks in Sicily.

I follow Milo around the bay until we come to the opening of an underwater cavern below the surface. Milo treads water. "Anita told me about this grotto here, and I thought it would be fun to explore it together."

I swallow hard, looking into the darkness below the surface of the water. I'm a little claustrophobic and the thought of diving under the water to get into a small cavern freaks me out.

"Don't tell me you're scared of caverns too, angel?"

I nod my head. "I don't like small spaces."

He wraps an arm around my waist, treading water effortlessly. "It'll be beautiful in there, and I won't let anything happen to you. I promise. I'll protect you."

Milo's promises shouldn't mean anything to me. Instead, his promise makes butterflies flutter to life in the pit of my stomach.

"What do you say?"

I nod in response. "Okay, let's do it."

He smiles that unnaturally beautiful smile at me. "Do you want to go first, or should I?"

I bite the inside of my cheek. "You first, and I'll follow close behind."

Milo nods, squeezing my hand before diving down into the dark hole ahead of us. I draw in a deep breath before following him. It's hard to keep my eyes open in the saltwater as we swim five meters to the other side of the rock formation and come up inside a small cavern that sparkles with the light penetrating through areas in the rock.

"Wow, this is amazing." I twirl around, thankful I can safely stand up in the cave. A fish bumps into my leg, making me jump.

"It's not as big as the Thunderball Grotto, which is a popular tourist attraction, but it'll do."

"Do for what?" I ask.

The expression on his face answers my question. I should have known he only brought me here for one thing. It's frustrating that an ache starts deep inside of me every time he looks at me like that.

Milo wades toward me and grabs me forcefully. "Anything I desire, princess."

I can't explain why that nickname makes my blood boil every time he says it. "I thought we were here to explore."

I feel him smile against the back of my neck. "That's right, explore each other," he purrs into my ear.

I shake my head, wrapping my arms around myself. "I don't feel like it right now."

Milo laughs that cruel, vindictive laugh for the first

time since we got here. "Since when do you think I care what you feel like?"

His comment slams into my gut hard, making my eyes water.

This trip has lured me into a trap. I'd allowed myself to wonder whether Milo could be kind and caring in our marriage, but it's all been one big act.

I spin around and step backward, placing some distance between us in the cavern. "Why do you have to be so cruel?" I shake my head, wishing my throat didn't close the moment our eyes met. His ice-blue eyes hold an unreadable coldness that I can hardly fathom. "This trip has made me realize you have the capacity for kindness, so why do you want to be so forceful with me?"

Milo smirks at me, and it makes my stomach drop. "You realize that this trip was an act to make it seem like we are a real couple." He shrugs. "I'm sorry if you got the impression this is how our life together would be, as it couldn't be farther from the truth." He steps closer to me, stinging me with every one of his vindictive words. "Your purpose as my wife is to please me and provide me with an heir, that's all."

It feels like Milo is tearing me apart. Our few fleeting days on this island have all been a lie, and that hurts more than I care to admit. Part of me wondered if I could find something good within Milo. It was a foolish notion, and I'm glad he's putting me right before my feelings get out of hand.

"Now, I want you to bend over," he orders, pinning

me to the spot with his cruel gaze. This is my life now. I'm nothing more than a slave to tend to his needs. He warned me about that the moment we met, and yet I foolishly believed that this could blossom into something more.

Hatred is a complicated feeling, and it easily blurs when you have to sleep with the guy you hate so much. His touch has become my addiction. When I don't move, he grabs my neck forcefully. "I told you to bend over, angel. Are you going to make me repeat myself?"

I feel the pain clutching around my chest as I shake my head, bending over slowly for him. His hands tease over my back first before traveling lower. "Good girl," he purrs.

I'm torn as my body responds to his touch, but my heart recoils. The hatred I held for him returns with a vengeance at his utter disrespect for me. Milo is crueler than I expected. He's playing games with my heart, and he doesn't care if I get hurt in the process.

He drags aside my bikini bottoms and thrusts his fingers inside of me.

Tears prickle at my eyes as I realize how utterly pathetic I've been on this trip, allowing him to infect my heart like a disease.

"I'm going to fuck your perfect little cunt when I want, do you understand?"

I swallow the pain clawing at my throat but don't respond to him.

My lack of response earns me a hard spank. The

pain helps to redirect my focus as I try desperately not to break in front of him. I can't let him know how deeply he has affected me.

"I asked you a question, princess. I want an answer."

"Yes, sir," I reply, hating how raw and broken my voice sounds.

He growls, and the sound reverberates around the cavern. "I told you when we're alone that you call me daddy."

The word feels too intimate for him. A man as cruel as he is doesn't deserve a name that should be linked to a protective and caring individual. Upon arriving here, I've researched his kinks, and he leans toward BDSM. I guess it's to be expected from a man as sick and twisted as him, but he most certainly isn't a Daddy Dom.

He's too cruel. I can only assume he enjoys the power play. The word makes him feel powerful.

My body tenses as I feel his finger pressing at my asshole. It's an odd sensation, and I instantly recoil, moving forward to get away from him. Milo reads my intention and grabs my hips just before I can get away. "Where do you think you're going, angel?"

I swallow hard, wishing I hadn't dived into this cavern with Milo. He's a monster. "I feel claustrophobic in here," I lie.

Milo grabs the back of my neck forcefully. "Stop your whining," he growls before thrusting a finger inside my ass and making me squeal in pain. "All I want to hear is you moaning as I fuck you."

It's the first time he's penetrated my ass, and he didn't even warn me. Slowly, he moves his finger in and out. Initially, it hurts, but gradually it starts to feel good. "I can't wait until I fuck this tight ass."

I tense at the thought of Milo's huge size in my ass.

He chuckles. "Don't worry. I won't do it here as it won't go in without some stretching."

The pain clutching around my heart fades away as I ignore it, knowing that Milo doesn't care what I want. I let my guard down around him on this island, which was a foolish mistake.

I bite my lip as he fucks my ass with his fingers, keeping silent. The last thing I want is to give this sadist satisfaction.

He spanks my sore ass. "I want to hear you moan. Your pussy is getting wet for me while I finger your ass, so don't pretend you aren't enjoying it."

This man's confidence is beyond cocky. Irritatingly, he's right. My body is incapable of self-control. Milo's touch is addictive. I shut my eyes and allow the sensations his touch ignites to overwhelm my senses, trying to forget how much Milo's hot-and-cold act hurts.

I should never have allowed this man to get under my skin. Milo grabs hold of my hips so hard it hurts and slides his thick cock deep inside of me, fucking me roughly. "Moan for me," he says slowly and forcefully.

I swallow my pride. Milo won't stop, not even if I

begged him to. He doesn't care about me or anyone other than himself. I shut my eyes and give in to the sensations he's teasing from my body. The moan that escapes me is strangled and emotional as tears escape my eyes, flooding down my cheeks.

"Good girl," he purrs.

It's ridiculous that a part of me swells with pride at his praise. As though I'm a little girl craving this cruel man's approval.

Milo fucks me harder. "I love fucking this perfect pussy. It's as though it was made to fit around my cock."

I grit my teeth, wishing his words didn't affect me the way they do. It's no use. I'm already hooked on Milo. Of all the dangers I thought I'd face when I was married to this monster, forming an attachment to him wasn't one I anticipated.

I try to detach myself from my thoughts, drowning instead in the unparalleled pleasure he so effortlessly coaxes from me. "Fuck, daddy," I moan, warning him that I'm close. It feels less natural than before and forced.

Perhaps it's because I know Milo will never feel anything for me. I'm nothing more than a fuck doll to him. He told me that much himself, and he's never given me a reason to believe it will ever be different between us. I was a fool to think there could be more between us.

16

MILO

The harshness of reality hits me the moment I step into my mansion. Piero is waiting for me with a look on his face that tells me we have trouble. After what happened at the wedding with Donatello's men, I shouldn't have been swanning off abroad. I should have been bringing him to his fucking knees.

Aida trails behind me quietly. She's been different ever since I snapped and treated her so cruelly in the cave off the beach. She can barely look me in the eye. The trip to the Bahamas was dangerous, as it showed her a side of me that can't exist here in Boston, no matter how much she wishes it did. The weight of the empire I hold on my shoulders makes it impossible.

Ever since our tour around the island, she had looked at me differently. I would say she looked at me with admiration. That was something I needed to extinguish before it grew into something dangerous. I hurt her in that cave, even if it hurt to do it to her. I had to do it for myself, as I too felt something I never should have for her. The start of something I never knew could feel. Care for another human being.

Aida is better off hating me and being forced to obey. She can't develop feelings for me, since a woman who wants more from me will only face disappointment. I can't give her what she wants. Aida desires a tenderness a man like me doesn't have the capacity for.

Piero stands to one side with his hands behind his back.

"What is it, Piero?" I ask before he even greets me.

He looks at Aida and then back at me. "It might be best if we talk in private."

I shake my head. "Whatever you want to say you can say it in front of my wife."

Piero swallows and nods. "We've run into some problems with the McCarthy clan since you left. They held up one of our drug deliveries at the port, and now it's gone missing."

"The fucking Irish." I run a hand through my hair and try to think quickly. "You're sure it was McCarthy?"

Malachy and I have a tentative agreement to keep out of each other's way. I'm not sure why he'd decide to break the agreement unless his men worked independently of his orders.

"We know that three of the men on the watch that night were his guys." Piero shrugs. "Two of them are in the basement and won't talk, but we're quietly confident they snatched the shipping container."

I glance behind me at Aida. The confident and fiery fight has left my angel, and it's a little disappointing that she didn't last longer. "Aida, go to your room," I order.

She doesn't look up at me or say a word as she moves past me and up the stairs. It irritates me that she didn't reply, but I haven't got time to scold her.

"Take me to them, now." As we walk down the corridor, I run a hand across the back of my neck. "What about Brando Donatello?"

Piero stiffens at the mention of my ex-girlfriend's father. "We are working on bringing him down too."

"Where are you with it, though?"

Piero shrugs. "They aren't stupid. They have been keeping their heads down ever since your wedding."

I crack my neck, irritated that I didn't just put off the honeymoon and go after him and his daughter that night. They will pay for it, but first I have to deal with the Irish rotting in my basement.

Piero leads me down the stairs, into the basement. I'm pissed off that anyone would dare steal a drug shipment from me. McCarthy may be Irish and an enemy for all intents and purpose, but he doesn't strike me as an idiot.

He wouldn't risk a war between his clan and my organization for two-and-a-half tons of cocaine. It may be worth a small fortune to most, near one-hundred million dollars, but it's not a lot in our world. It still angers me, though.

"Do you know their names?"

Piero nods. "Yes, sir. One is Dillion Kelly, and the other is Sean Walsh." He shrugs. "They're low-level runners in McCarthy's clan, as far as we can tell. We found footage of them taking the container away with a lorry. I have not found the driver."

I clench my fists. "Make sure we have all resources trying to find the driver and the container. Then I want you to set up a meeting with Malachy."

"Are you sure that's a good idea, sir? Remember what happened last time you met."

I remember what happened the last time the two of us were in the same room. Both of us are too proud to back down, and we ended up in a fistfight, which Malachy won. He's an undefeated bare-knuckle fighter. His victory led to me agreeing to the tentative truce between his clan and my mafia.

"I'm sure. We need to find out if these guys were working independently from Malachy or not. If these assholes won't tell us the truth, then it's the only way."

Piero looks uncertain, but he knows not to question me again. "Okay, shall I leave you with them?"

I nod in response and enter the holding cell we use to keep our prisoners locked away.

One man is hanging by his arms in the corner. They stripped the other naked, and he is slumped in a chair in the center of the room. They beat his face up, and there's blood coating the floor beneath him.

I crack my neck and ready myself. This situation is the polar opposite of lounging in a villa in the Bahamas with my wife. Normally, I enjoy taking matters into my own hands, but it feels different after getting back home with Aida.

I groan internally, wondering if I'm going soft.

What has Aida done to me?

Our trip away together was the first time I've had fun since I was a kid. Even then, life wasn't a picnic with an abusive father and a mother who couldn't stand up to him.

My mother used to take me on outings, but my father would be angry that she took me out of the house when we returned. He used to beat her regularly in front of me. Maybe that's why I'm so fucked up.

I shake my head, trying to focus my mind. There are torture implements on a table to the right, and I grab a sharp but small knife, twisting the blade between my fingers.

"Time to wake up, motherfuckers," I shout, bringing the two assholes out of the stupor they'd fallen into.

The guy in the chair sees me and instantly pisses himself. My reputation for torture is renowned across the city. They may be Irish, but they'll know who I am.

"That's fucking pathetic." I approach him and drag the small knife over his skin gently, teasing at what is coming. "I think you should tell me who stole my drugs for before that puddle beneath you becomes blood rather than piss."

He meets my gaze and doesn't speak.

"I would start speaking if I were you." I slice the skin from his arm, making him squeal like a woman.

"Fuck," he says, shaking his head. "I can't take this anymore. I'll tell you who it was."

The other guy hung up by his shoulders shouts for him to stop. "Don't do it, Dillion. You know he will kill us for ratting him out."

I laugh at that idiotic notion. "Neither of you are leaving my home alive. You can tell me now, and I'll make your death quick and painless, or I can drag it out for many painful weeks."

There's a deathly silence that falls across the room before the guy who originally spoke nods. "Fine, we were working for Mikhail Gurin."

Fucking Russians. I should have known they were behind this attack. My meeting won't be necessary, but I'll need to tell him I killed two of his men for screwing me. Honesty is best on this occasion.

"Thank you for coming clean." I walk around the back of his chair and slide my arm around his neck, snapping it quickly.

I had no intention of breaking my word to this man, but the other man is another story. He didn't tell me what I wanted to know so he will suffer a slow and painful death.

"You tried to stop him from telling me the truth, which means your death will be torturous."

The guy opens his busted-up eye and looks me in the eye. "Do your worst."

He's strong, unlike his friend. It is a trait I admire, and it makes sense why he's the one hanging up by his arms.

"At least you will not die a coward like that sad bastard." I nod at his dead friend's lifeless body.

He narrows his eyes at me. "Never. I'll die with my pride intact, you sick fuck."

I smirk at that. "Probably best not to insult the man who is going to take his time slowly torturing you." I twirl the knife in my hand and approach him, recognizing the glint of fear that ignites in his eyes.

He is fighting to stay strong, but no man can hold out until the end. Malachy may not appreciate the murder of these two men, whose positions in his clan I'm not sure of. I grab his hand and slide the end of the thin knife into his fingertip.

"Motherfucker," he growls.

I pull the knife out and stab it into his next fingertip. It's one of the most painful points in the body because there are so many neurons. They are the perfect weak spot to exploit, but many people don't think of using them while torturing.

You can't put the body through too many serious injuries and sustain life, so finding areas of the body that provide the most pain with the least damage is the key.

He grunts as I thrust the knife into the end of his third fingertip. I'm surprised how resilient he is, as many men would crack from the level of pain.

The guy grits his teeth so hard I can almost hear the enamel grinding off. It's a satisfying sound, as I know he's slowly breaking. I get to his next finger and stab it in as far as I can until I hit the bone.

This time he cries out in a deep, rasping expression of pain. By the time I'm through with each finger, he'll be a mess. A flashback of my father committing the same torture to a young boy, no older than eighteen, after he fucked up a deal with a wealthy Italian family from New York, the D'Angelos, springs into my mind. I was about fifteen years old, and my father stood where I stand now, teaching me the perfect way to inflict pain.

My father taught me his ruthless ways from an early age. First with his treatment of my mother, but later by involving me in his work. It desensitized me to violence, but he also taught me to enjoy torturing victims.

"Stop, please," Sean rasps, eyes wild with fear as he allows the pain to break his resolve.

I smirk at him begging me. "Perhaps you're a coward after all." His fingertips are bloody, except for the last two on his left hand. He had pretty good stamina to withstand the torture to that point.

"Fuck you," he spits, shaking his head. "I didn't beg the first eight times."

The guy is made of far sterner stuff than his friend.

"True. You can rest for now until I decide to punish you more." I turn away from him. Quickly, I turn back around and punch him hard in the gut. The guy grunts, unable to protect himself because he's hung from the ceiling. "Don't think I'm soft, though, you son of a bitch."

He spits blood onto the floor, which is a satisfying sight. The torture my men already put him through has done some internal damage, which will mean his pain is continuous. I turn away from my victim without another word and walk out of the basement.

Piero is waiting dutifully outside. "Is it done, sir?"

I shake my head. "One is dead, the other I wish to torture for longer." I run a hand across the back of my neck. "I need you to get me a lead on Donatello, though."

Piero's brow furrows. "Is it wise to chase after them when the Irish are attacking us?"

The mere thought of letting what Donatello's men did at the wedding slide makes my skin crawl. "I want my revenge for what they did. In what world would I let that slide?"

Piero shrugs. "I merely meant it may be safer to wait to get your revenge."

"No, I want to know how to hit back at him. Get me my angle in three days." I glare at my capo who clearly disapproves.

"Fine, I'll work on it."

"Good," I say, leaving without another word. He

can clean up the mess I made. Piero knows me and he knows I wouldn't just wait to get my revenge after such a blatant attack.

The Bahamas was a short escape from reality, but this is who I am. I can't forget that. My entire empire could fall if I don't rule with an iron fist.

I won't let Aida get in the way of that. A weakness was trying to infect me, but I won't risk everything my father built over some questionable feelings for Aida.

The honeymoon is over. Now it's time to show her who I really am.

17

AIDA

"How do you like this dress, Mrs. Mazzeo?" Olivia asks, holding up a stunning pale blue evening gown with silver lace detailing.

Olivia offered to help me get ready for the charity event, which we're leaving for in an hour.

"It's beautiful."

Olivia smiles. "Why don't you try it on? It will look even more stunning on you, Mrs. Mazzeo."

I shake my head and place a hand on her arm. "How many times do I have to tell you to call me Aida?"

"Sorry, Aida. It's a habit that isn't easy to shake." She passes the dress into my hands. "I can't call you that around Mr. Mazzeo, though. He wouldn't approve."

I nod. "I have a deal, then. Anytime we're alone,

you'll call me Aida." I smile at her. "If Milo is around, you can call me Mrs. Mazzeo."

She sighs a breath of relief. "Sounds like a good plan."

I'm thankful to have Olivia around as she's friendly and the closest thing I have to a friend here in Boston. All my life, Gia, Siena, and I have been inseparable. It feels like a part of me was torn away when my father shipped me over here. I may not be able to speak so freely with Olivia, but I'm thankful to have someone to talk to.

"How long have you worked for Milo?" I ask, stripping my dressing gown off and unzipping the stunning evening gown to try on. It feels as expensive as it looks.

She clears her throat. "Seven years I've worked for Mr. Mazzeo. He's a fair employer." I get a hint of discomfort in her tone, talking about Milo at all.

I pull the dress up and turn around. "Could you zip me up?" I ask.

"Of course." She rushes over and pulls the zipper up on the dress.

I sigh heavily. "I find it hard to believe Milo is a fair anything. He's certainly not a fair husband."

Olivia gasps slightly. "Don't let him hear you say that about him."

I shake my head. "He knows my sentiments for him."

I turn around to gauge Olivia's reaction to the dress. Her mouth falls open. "Wow, you look..." She shakes her head. "I don't know how to put it into words." She ushers me to the mirror, and I look at myself in it. She's right. The dress looks good.

"Maybe that's why you can get away with telling Milo what you think of him." Olivia's eyes widen, and she presses a hand to her mouth. "I mean Mr. Mazzeo." She shakes her head. "In the seven years I've worked here, I've never called him that." She laughs. "I think you're a bad influence on me, Aida."

I laugh at that. "Sorry. At least Milo isn't here to hear it."

"Isn't here to hear what?" A deep, baritone voice speaks from behind us, making us jump.

Olivia pales as she turns around to face her employer, who she's scared of. I guess it makes sense, considering he's a mob boss. Most people must find him scary, but I've grown up around men like him my entire life.

I shake my head. "We were chatting about my dress."

Milo's eyes narrow, and he drags them down my body. The desire that ignites in his eyes almost burns me. It's hot and passionate. "It's a beautiful dress, angel, but you know I don't like you to lie to me."

I glance briefly at Olivia, who looks like she is about to pass out. "Fine, Olivia mentioned you're a fair employer, and I said I find it hard to believe you're a fair anything. You are certainly not a fair husband." I tilt my head to the side slightly as I notice his jaw clench. "She told me not to let you hear me say it." I shrug. "Now you have."

"Leave us, Olivia," Milo orders, never once taking his eyes from me.

She bows her head and gives me a thankful glance. There was no way I would get her in trouble with this psychopath because she called him by his name.

I turn my back on my husband and look into the mirror again, making sure my hair is presentable. "You don't look like you're ready for the event tonight," I point out since his hair is ruffled and he's wearing the same shirt and pants he wore on the plane.

Milo appears behind me in the mirror, and the look in his eyes is deadly. "You don't speak to my staff about me, do you understand?" He grabs hold of my hips hard, digging his fingertips in.

I glare at him in the mirror, hating the man who thinks he can take whatever he wants. The man who thinks he owns me. It's the first time he's spoken to me since he fucked me in the cave. I hate having him touch me, but my treacherous body loves it.

It feels like I'm being torn in two by my mind and body, each wanting different things.

He bites the exposed skin on my neck. "I asked you a question."

I grind my teeth together before answering him. "Yes, I understand."

A beast-like rumble rises in his chest. "Yes, what?"

The bastard can't leave it at that. He must push me

every step of the way. "I answered your question. What is your problem?"

He grabs hold of my throat from behind and pushes me hard against the mirror. "How many times do I have to tell you not to push me?" I feel his hand lift the skirt of my gown to expose my ass to him. He spanks me hard, making me yelp. "Bad girls need to be punished, and you're not following the rules."

I don't say anything, glaring at him in the glass he has me pressed against.

"I want to hear you say it."

I know what he wants to hear, but my mind recoils at the thought. Although I called him daddy in the Bahamas and before, it feels unnatural because of how his words hurt me in the grotto. Sir is detached and clinical, but daddy feels too intimate with a man whose heart is made of ice.

"I understand, sir," I grit out.

Milo nips my earlobe with his teeth. "We're alone, angel, which means I want you to call me by a different name."

"Oh, of course. Yes, I understand, you pig," I spit, feeling the anger for this man spiral out of control. He may have all the power here, but it doesn't mean I have to make things easy for him. If he wanted a woman that would lay down and take everything that he gives her without complaint, he should have married a hooker.

He turns me around and looms over me angrily.

"You're testing my patience, little girl, and I don't have time for this."

I shrug. "No, we're going to be late. So why don't you get dressed and leave me alone?"

Milo punches the mirror above me hard enough to crack it, making me jump. I glance up at the shattered mirror and see Milo's knuckles are bleeding.

"Cazzo, come nascondi la ferita?" I ask him how he will hide the wound in Italian.

He tightens his grip on my hips and forces me to look at him. "I don't need to hide it, angel. I need you to do as you're told." Despite the fit of rage I witnessed, the only thing I detect in his eyes is desire.

"Go and fetch the first aid kit from the bathroom," he says.

I nod, but he doesn't let me go.

"Say it, bella," he pushes.

I swallow my pride, knowing when to admit defeat. Milo doesn't strike me as the kind of guy that would have any qualms about hitting me. Thankfully, the mirror was the only casualty today. "Yes, daddy," I say, but there's a tone of irritation in my voice.

Milo lets me go. "Good girl," he purrs.

It annoys me that every time he calls me that, my thighs tremble and my pussy gets wet. Anytime he's an asshole to me, I find it a turn-on. There's something wrong with me for wanting such a vindictive man.

I escape from his grasp and rush into the bathroom, grabbing the first aid kit under the sink. When I return,

Milo is stripped naked. It's impossible not to stare at his muscular, tattooed body that makes my mouth dry and my pussy drip.

"Quit gawping, angel, and bring me the kit. I need to patch up my hand."

I feel heat flood my cheeks as I bring the kit to him. "Should I?"

He looks at me for a few beats before nodding.

I open the kit and take out the saline solution, cleaning the wound first.

Milo doesn't bat an eyelid or flinch when I pat the wound. It's as if he feels nothing. I make quick work of bandaging the cuts on his knuckles. Milo doesn't say anything as I pack away the kit. Instead, he walks into the bathroom and turns on the faucet in the shower.

I take the kit and place it back under the sink. "The bandages aren't waterproof, so don't get them wet."

Milo glares at me. "I'm not stupid, princess. Watch it, or I'll be putting you in here with me to suck me off."

"I've already showered. Shall I get a tuxedo out of the closet ready for you?" I ask.

He nods in response, stepping under the spray of the water.

I linger for a few moments, watching the way his muscles tense and contract. He's the most attractive man I've ever seen, naked or dressed. Sometimes it's hard to match his beautiful appearance to his rotten personality. I walk back into our room and through the door into our dressing room.

Milo has about seven tuxedos hung up and countless numbers of suits. I select a black tuxedo and white shirt, along with a black bow tie. Something tells me that Milo will look irresistible in a tux like he looked irresistible in the suit he wore to our wedding. I lay the outfit on the bed as the faucet in the bathroom shuts off.

He returns to the bedroom with the towel hanging loosely on his muscled hips. I keep my gaze away from him as he slides on a pair of clean boxers and then proceeds to get dressed.

He's silent as he gets ready before turning to me when he's ready. "Come on, peeping beauty. We're going to be late."

I glare at him. "I wasn't peeping. I was looking away to give you privacy."

He laughs. "I wasn't talking about while I was getting dressed. I was talking about while I was showering." He smirks at me. "I saw you in the reflection of the tiles watching me." He winks and it makes my blood boil.

"You're a pig," I say, jumping up from the seat and strutting toward the door.

He grabs me before I exit. "Am I now? I'll show you how much of a pig I am when I get you back here after this event, angel, don't you worry." He slides his hands down from my waist to my hips. "I've told you before, don't turn your back on me. I expect you to behave tonight, or your punishment will be unbearable." He pulls down my panties and shoves two thick fingers inside of me. "So fucking wet," he growls.

He pulls out a pair of panties from his suit jacket pocket and thrusts them at me. "Put these on before we leave."

I look at him quizzically.

"They're vibrating panties. I want to have some fun with my disobedient little brat tonight."

I shake my head. "No chance."

He tightens his grip on my hips, so it hurts. "It's not a request. It's an order."

Reluctantly, I grab the panties and swap them over, feeling painfully aware that he can turn them on at any time he chooses.

I let out a shaky breath, hating the way my thighs clench at the promise of punishment from his hand. I can't understand why I want a man who degrades me in this way, but it seems his cruel dominance is all it takes to get me wet between my thighs. I guess this is why I always felt attracted to the story's villain rather than the hero.

18

MILO

*A*ida fights me every step of the way. For some sick reason, I love it. Our marriage wouldn't be half as enjoyable if she had no fire or fight to her. It's sick that I want her to fight, but I am sick.

The moment we stepped into this ballroom, she changed. The easy facade she put in place at our wedding reception returns, and she acts like a doting wife while wearing the panties I made her wear. I have the controller for them in my suit jacket. Tonight will be fun.

I watch as she laughs with the mayor, fitting this life like a missing piece of the puzzle. I haven't told her, but she looks gorgeous in the turquoise blue and silver evening gown she selected tonight. Every man has looked at her in this room more than once, and it makes me feel possessive.

I'd rather she was wrapped up in some shabby dress

that no man would look at her in. She's better at this than I am, as I sip a glass of whiskey by the bar and watch her.

I find these people insufferable. They're pathetic. All of them were born with a silver spoon in their mouths. They know nothing about suffering to get what you want.

My life has been a fight from the moment I was brought screaming into this world. I'll never stop fighting. On the other hand, Aida is so cool and collected, even when she's challenging me. It's as though nothing can scare her, or at least that's what she wants me to believe.

"Milo, how was the honeymoon?" Michael King's voice makes my muscles tense. He's the last guy I want to talk to right now.

"It was fine," I reply, knocking back the rest of my scotch and slamming the glass down on the bar. I catch the bartender's gaze and signal for another.

Michael laughs. "Just fine? I'm sure it was amazing with that smoking hot—"

I grab hold of Michael's collar and push him hard against the bar, making people around us gasp in surprise. "Finish that fucking sentence, and I'll knock those new, shiny teeth out," I growl.

Michael pales, holding his hands up. "Sorry, Milo. I was only complimenting your wife."

I clench my jaw, knowing these stuck-up assholes won't tolerate aggression. "Well, don't. Aida's my wife, and I don't want other men gawping at her." I let go of his collar and grab my scotch. "Stay away from my wife, King." I walk toward Aida.

She notices me approaching, and there's a look of annoyance in her eyes as I wrap an arm around her. "There you are, angel. I wondered where you had gotten to," I purr.

Patricia claps her hands. "Oh, you do make an adorable couple," she says, the cynicism detectable in her voice. Her jealousy is ugly, especially since she's a married woman.

"Indeed. Did you enjoy the Bahamas?" Thomas asks.

I nod. "It was nice to have a break."

Thomas nods. "Yes, you work too hard. Aida, did you like the Bahamas?"

Aida glances briefly at me before answering. "It's a beautiful paradise, and I loved every moment of it. The island reminds me a little of my homeland, Sicily, which I miss very much." I know that if she were given a chance to go back to Sicily, she'd take it without a second thought.

"Well, we best do our rounds," I say to the mayor.

He shakes his head. "No way. We haven't even seen any of the pictures of your trip."

For fuck's sake, this is why I knew I needed to take photos. "Of course. Aida has them on her phone."

Her brow furrows as she pulls her cell phone out of her clutch and navigates to her photos. "Yes, it looks like

I do." She glares at me for a second before passing the phone to Thomas. "I would recommend visiting the Exumas. They're magical."

Patricia looks at the photos, smiling falsely. "Maybe that should be our next holiday destination, Thomas?" she suggests.

Thomas nods. "It does look particularly beautiful." He passes the phone back to Aida. "I'm glad you had a lovely time. You'll both need to come over to our place for dinner sometime."

Dinner invitations to the mayor's home are few and far between. Thomas must like Aida, since I've never been invited to their home. "That would be such an honor, Thomas," I reply, knowing that if I want to keep solidifying my position within this city and secure a seat on the city council, this is the path to take.

Thomas smiles and nods. "Perfect. I'll get my secretary to set it up with yours."

"Sounds wonderful," Aida says, smiling at Thomas.

I get the feeling that my wife's stunning looks might have something to do with Thomas wanting her around. If that's true, then so be it. As long as he doesn't try anything with her, it's fine if it gets me where I want to be.

"I'll let you both mingle now," Thomas says. "See you both soon."

I guide Aida away from him, and once we're out of earshot, I speak. "Well done, Aida. I've been trying to get invited to that assholes home for about three years.

You meet him twice, and suddenly we're invited over as guests to the mayor's home."

Aida glances at me. "You think he only invited us because of me?"

Her innocence is endearing.

"I'm pretty sure the mayor likes what he sees."

Aida stops walking and steps out of my grasp. "Are you saying that you're alright with another man objectifying me if it gets you what you want?"

I sigh heavily, realizing that saying anything at all was a mistake. Aida takes offense to almost everything I say, even when it's not meant to offend.

"Don't get your panties in a bunch, angel. He would never get a chance to touch you."

Aida looks even angrier. "I should fucking well hope not."

I grab her wrist and pull her close to me. "Don't make a scene here, angel, and don't make me wash your mouth out with soap. I don't want to hear another dirty word out of that mouth of yours until we're back in our bed. Do you hear me?"

Aida glares at me and yanks her hand from my grasp, turning and walking away from me toward the bathroom.

I grab the controller out of my jacket pocket and turn it on.

Aida yelps in surprise and stops walking. She glances back at me in shock before rushing faster out of the hall.

This woman is testing my last nerve. First she was disobedient back at home, and now here. I need to teach her a good lesson. She needs to be forced into submission as I make her come in a room full of people, controlling those panties all night.

I follow her calmly out of the main hall of the event and into the bathroom.

Aida turns around and glares at me. "You can't be in here," she says, crossing her arms over her chest. "And you should turn that fucking thing off."

I tilt my head and smirk at her. "Can't is a really bad choice of word when it comes to me." I turn the lock on the door, and Aida pales.

I stalk toward her and set a hand on either side of her on the counter. "You aren't a very quick learner, are you?"

She bites her bottom lip, looking up at me. "I think it's more a matter of I don't want to learn."

I grab her chin forcefully, digging my nails into her skin. "Wrong answer, angel. I'm going to torment you all night for your disobedience. It's time for dinner. We need to get to our table."

Aida's eyes flash with fear for the first time in a while. "Dinner?"

I nod, smiling at her. "Yes, we will be at a table with eight others, and these panties will not be turning off tonight." I slide a hand up her thigh and dip my fingers under the fabric of the vibrating panties, finding her already soaking wet. "So wet for me. I bet you're gagging for my cock to fill you up."

She glares at me again, the fear fading away. "You wish," she says.

I laugh. "By the time we get back home, you will be begging me for it, princess." I pull my finger out of her and hold it up, then slide it into my mouth and suck her sweet juices from it.

Even though she's angry at me, her eyes dilate at the sight of me tasting her like that.

"Now, we don't want people to wonder where we are. Come on." I drag her back into the events room, where people are already sat at their tables. I find our table and hold out her seat for her, which she sits in.

The panties are only on a low setting now, but I intend to punish Aida for her disobedience. There's no better punishment than making her come in front of people she doesn't know.

"Milo, I heard your honeymoon was idyllic from the mayor. Can I see the photos?" Jameson asks. He's one of the council members.

I nod and nudge Aida under the table, who is already looking suitably flushed. "Aida, can you show Jameson the photos, please?"

She nods. "Of course. Here you go." She passes her unlocked cell phone over the table. Her voice is surprisingly steady, considering our little secret buzzing between her thighs. I reach into my pocket and turn the setting up one.

Aida jolts in her seat, clenching her jaw.

"Wonderful photos. Do you recommend the Exumas after visiting, Aida?" Jameson asks.

I smirk at the uncomfortable look on Aida's face. "Definitely," she replies, taking her cell phone back and placing it in her clutch. I turn the vibrator up another notch, and she cries out suddenly.

The guest at the table looks at her quizzically. "Are you feeling okay, Aida?" Alice, another one of the council members, asks.

She nods. "Yes, I felt a bit strange for a moment there." Aida glares at me.

Alice's brow furrows, but her attention is drawn to the stage as the mayor speaks. This charity event is an auction, which means people won't focus on my dirty little wife coming in her panties.

Aida is squirming in her seat now, and her cheeks are practically crimson.

I lean toward her. "I'd sit back and enjoy it if I were you. Fighting it is a bad idea," I mutter.

She grabs hold of my cock and squeezes. I think she was aiming for the balls to hurt me, but all it does is make me harder.

"I told you that you'd be desperate for my cock. I didn't think you'd be gagging for it this soon," I whisper into Aida's ear.

She whimpers softly before letting go and collapsing back in her chair. There's a euphoric look on her face as she gives in to the sensation and climaxes at the table. I reach for her under the table and feel the slickness between her thighs.

Satisfied, I turn the panties off to give her a break. She glares at me and sits up straight. "That was a real dick move," she says quietly.

I shake my head. "I told you no more dirty words out of your mouth until you're in my bed." With that, I turn the panties back on, and she cries out so loud half the room glances her way.

My naughty little wife wants to do things the hard way. I can't deny that I love having her at my mercy. The dominance I feel right now gives me a rush of adrenaline. I can't wait to fuck her later.

AIDA STORMS into the room and tears off her panties, chucking them on the floor. She's angry, and it's a real turn-on. "What the hell was that tonight?"

I lean against the door and watch her. "I told you that you'd regret disobeying me."

She shakes her head. "You made me look a fool. I came four times at the dinner table, and two times I couldn't keep quiet." She's exasperated, and it's sexy as hell.

I can't recall a time in my life that I've ever felt this much desire for a woman. She drives me crazy.

"I thought you wanted to make a good impression, but all you've done is make your wife look crazy."

I laugh at that. "Don't worry. I made an excuse that you caught some weird bug in the Bahamas and that you aren't feeling yourself."

She cries out in irritation and rushes toward the bathroom. "You're the most infuriating man I've ever met."

I see what's she's planning and stride over to the door, shoving my foot in before she can shut it on me. "There's no escaping me. That dripping wet pussy is ready for my cock, and I'm not going to deny it what it wants any longer."

I push the door open and walk toward her.

"I don't want you to fuck me." She backs away from me, stepping away with every step I take.

"You are a very bad liar, Aida Mazzeo. Also, it doesn't matter what you want." I back her against the glass of the shower cubicle, trapping her in with my hands. "It matters that I want to fuck you right now, and I own you." I use one hand to unzip my pants and free my cock, stroking it. "Now hold onto my shoulders."

As always, she defies me and keeps her hands by her sides. I lift her against the glass with one hand and position my cock beneath her. Slowly, I slide her soaking wet cunt over my cock. Every muscle clamps down around my shaft, and I grunt.

"That's it, Aida, take my cock like the naughty little brat you are."

She moans so loud that it makes my balls ache for

release. I've been desperate for her since before she grabbed my cock under the table. I thrust into her, fucking her against the shower pane like an animal that's lost all control.

"Fuck, yes," she cries out. Aida's futile attempts to deny she wants me are non-existent. Her arms lock around my neck as she helps me, bobbing up and down on my cock harder and faster.

We've both lost control as I take her without mercy. Every time we've gotten intimate up to now, I've played with her first. Granted, the entire charity event I was "playing" with her, but there's something more desperate and passionate about this moment.

"Oh, daddy, I'm going to come," she whines, making my balls clench.

I feel myself explode deep inside of her as I continue to fuck her against the wall. "That's it, angel. Come on daddy's cock," I growl against her neck as her juices drip down my cock. I continue thrusting my hips into her hard and fast to drain every drop of my seed. That weird primal need to get her pregnant still rules me, and it's a sensation I can't comprehend.

Aida is an enigma to me. No woman has ever made me lose control like this, and it worries me more than anything. In all my life, I've never lost control. This woman has managed to unravel me in such a short time.

19

AIDA

A week has passed since we returned to Boston and attended the charity event. The event where Milo made me hate him and want him more than ever. It makes no sense, but my body craves his unapologetic dominance while my mind rejects it.

I've rarely seen him at all since that night as he has been busy with work. Anytime I do see him, he's cold and distant. He hasn't touched me since that night.

The moment we walked back into the mansion after getting off the plane, his man was waiting for him with a solemn look on his face. He mentioned that they were having troubles with the McCarthy clan, but that meant nothing to me. I have no idea about how things are run in Boston or who Milo's enemies are.

It frustrates me that part of me has been disappointed by the lack of time he's spent with me, especially since I should loathe him for the way he treats me.

For the first time since we returned, we had dinner together last night when the same man came in and cut it short. He wasn't very clear about the problem but said an emergency needed Milo's attention. I expected to be glad not to have to see Milo too often, but instead, I feel lonely.

He returned in the early hours of the morning and snuck into bed before leaving at six o'clock this morning. I believe he thought I was asleep on both occasions.

There's been an awkward tension between us ever since he lost control and fucked me against the shower after the charity event.

The time spent on the island felt like I was with a different man entirely. Maybe Milo has split personalities, as it sure felt like it at times. It's blurred the lines between us, and I've got no idea how to act around him.

I check my hair in the mirror before heading out of our room. Olivia is walking toward me as I step outside. "Mrs. Mazzeo, there's a parcel for you downstairs."

"Do you know who the parcel is from?" I ask, wondering who on earth could have sent a parcel addressed to me here

She shakes her head. "No, there's a card with it, but I have not touched it. The delivery guy dropped it off."

No one knows my address from my previous life, so I can only assume it's a late wedding gift from one of Milo's friends. I enter the dining room and see a large box wrapped in emerald wrapping paper.

Olivia follows me. "I'm intrigued about what is inside. Do you mind?"

I shake my head. "Of course not."

I reach for the ribbon around the parcel and open it, lifting the lid and glancing inside to see a green dress. It's expensive, and there's a hand-written note on top of it.

For an angel that deserves to be in heaven.

My brow furrows as I stare at the dress before pulling it out. My heart drops into my stomach as I hear what sounds like the ticking of a detonator. All my time with my dad taught me a trick or two. Oliva is fawning over the dress as I grab her hand, pulling her toward the nearest obstacle to cover us from the blast. I pull her behind the sofa.

"Aida, what are —"

She's cut short from asking her question as the blast shakes the room. Her eyes are wide as bits of the hardwood dining table splinter. A few of them land on us.

"Fuck. We need to call Mr. Mazzeo right away," she says. "If you hadn't realized there was a bomb in the parcel, we'd both be splattered across this damn room." Her body is shaking as she remains behind the sofa. "Fucking lucky."

I nod. "The moment I heard the ticking coming from the package, I knew."

A man comes running into the room, the same man that interrupted dinner with Milo last night. "Mrs. Mazzeo?" He sounds panicked.

I stand and reveal myself, and so does Olivia.

"Are you alright?" he asks, rushing over to me.

I nod. "Yes. Luckily, we're both fine."

Olivia is shaking. "Only thanks to Aida; she saved both of our lives."

"I'm Piero, and I work with Milo." He shoots a stern gaze at Olivia. "Who allowed this parcel inside the house?"

Olivia pales. "I believe Helen took the parcel in, but I brought it into the dining room for Mrs. Mazzeo. There was no way I could have known there was a bomb inside it."

Piero shakes his head. "We'll discuss this more later. For now, please leave us."

Olivia swallows hard before squeezing my hand and obeying his command.

Piero brings his hand up to my face. "You are hurt."

I touch my face and find my fingers bloody. "It's a scratch. Who sent the parcel?"

He walks toward the blown-up dress, which lays a few meters from the damaged oak table. "I have a good idea from the color of this dress. The Irish." He looks up at me. "Milo is on his way back as I told him there was an explosion. He will want a doctor to check you over in your room."

I stare at him, wondering why I'd need to see a doctor. "A doctor isn't necessary."

Piero clenches his jaw. "Please don't make this hard

on either of us. I will be in trouble if I don't get a doctor to check you over."

I nod, feeling a heaviness settle on my chest. "I understand." I walk out of the dining room and head toward my room.

Piero escorts me, making sure I do as he says and go to my room. Once there, he stands in the doorway. "The doctor will be here in five minutes. Stay put." He slams the door shut, making me jump.

I stare at the door in shock. It takes a few minutes until the reality of what happened sinks in. My stomach churns, and the tears start to flow freely. I could have died barely ten minutes ago.

I remember the lies Milo spoke before we dived into that grotto.

I won't let anything happen to you. I promise. I'll protect you.

Words that were a ploy to get me into that grotto with him. Milo doesn't care what happens to me, and he made that clear once we were inside. He is cruel, and despite his capacity for kindness, he chooses to treat me badly.

The shock of everything that has happened in the past couple of weeks hits me all at once. My father's betrayal, Milo's cruel ways, and now I've almost been blown to pieces in my husband's dining room.

My cell phone rings, and I'm surprised when I see it's a Sicilian number. I answer it instantly. "Hello."

"Aida, thank god. Gia and I have been trying to get hold of you for days. We were so worried."

I sigh a breath of relief, thankful to hear Siena's voice. "I know. Milo has blocked incoming calls from anyone saved in my phone."

"What a fucking asshole," Gia says.

I smile at that, wiping away the tears staining my cheeks. "Yeah, he is."

"Are you okay, though? You sound shook up," Siena asks.

I have no idea how to answer that question. I'm anything but okay. "Not really," I say, feeling my throat close.

Siena is the first to speak. "What's up?"

I shake my head, wondering why she has to ask that question. "I'm married to a monster and almost got blown up in his dining room. That's what is up."

Gia grabs the phone from Siena. "That was a stupid question. You almost got blown up? How?"

I shake my head even though they can't see me. "I don't know exactly. One of Milo's enemies tried to kill me."

"Oh my God. Are you uninjured?" Siena asks.

"Yes. I'm fine, just shook up."

Gia grabs the phone again. "Can we come and visit you yet? We need to give this husband of yours a piece of our minds."

I wish they could come and visit me, but I know Milo won't allow it. He didn't even allow my bodyguard to stay on, a man who could have proven helpful a moment ago when I was almost blown to pieces. "I don't think Milo will allow it."

"Fuck him," Siena says.

"Yeah, he can't stop us from seeing you for the rest of our lives," Gia adds.

They don't know what kind of man I'm married to. He can and will stop me from seeing my friends if he wants. "He can do what he wants and makes that clear to me whenever I don't follow his orders."

Gia clicks her tongue. "Sounds like a fucking asshole."

I laugh. "You can say that again." I sigh heavily, longing so badly to be back home. My father is an asshole, but I'd still return to Sicily in a heartbeat if I could. There wouldn't be a moment's hesitation. I miss my friends.

A knock at the door interrupts our conversation. "Sorry, guys, I've got to go."

Siena and Gia try to protest, but I cancel the call without another word. The last thing I need is for Milo to hear that my friends have found a way to contact me. His desire to block everything good out of my life makes me hate him more than I can explain. It infects my blood and makes me so angry I want to murder him.

"Come in," I answer the second knock.

A man who must be about fifty years old with graying hair enters the room. "Mrs. Mazzeo, I'm Doctor Allan Kingsley, and I've been instructed to check you over." His brow furrows. "I heard you had a close shave with a bomb only twenty minutes ago."

I nod in response.

"Mr. Mazzeo has requested I give you a medical check to ensure you are fine. Although, I am correct in assuming you sustained no wounds?"

"No wounds, only a few scratches from the debris on my arms." I point at the cuts on my arm.

He sets his bag down on the dresser and gets out a stethoscope and blood pressure monitor. "I'll check your blood pressure first. Can you take your cardigan off?"

I shrug the cardigan off, and he affixes the monitor to my left arm. The tests seem like overkill considering I wasn't hurt.

The doctor does his tests, writing down notes. "You're all clear, Aida. I'd say you may be in a bit of shock, though, as your blood pressure was elevated." He packs away his instruments. "Just take it easy for the rest of the day."

"Okay, thank you." I sit back on the bed as he lets himself out.

I sigh and rest my head back on the pillow. Ever since I got back from the Bahamas, it's been an emotional rollercoaster, and the bomb is the icing on the cake. Things can only get worse from here, not better.

20

MILO

*B*lood paints the air as my fist connects with his face. "Tell me why your father attacked me at my own wedding," I growl.

Marcus Donatello glares at me through a busted eye. "I have no idea."

"Liar," I growl, punching him hard in the gut. "Do you want to die here?"

Marcus draws in a shaky breath. "My father will kill you for this."

I laugh at the ridiculous notion that Brando Donatello has the power to even touch me. "Your father is nothing. He's weak and pathetic." I circle around the young heir to the Donatello business. "Tell me the truth."

Marcus searches my eyes, as if looking for a shred of mercy. He won't find any of that from me. I have no mercy for my enemies. "It wasn't my father that organized the sabotage of your wedding."

I know that he's lying. It's pathetic how bad at it he is.

"Carmella was behind it." He shrugs. "She's jealous that you moved on and got married, while she's alone and miserable."

I narrow my eyes at him. "Isn't that just an easy way to acquit yours and your father's guilt? Pinning it on my ex-girlfriend?"

He shakes his head. "I swear it."

I punch him in the gut again, making him grunt. "You're a bad liar. Lorenzo works for your father. He wouldn't betray your father's trust just to help your sister."

Marcus spits out blood. "Fine. My father thinks you made a mockery of our family when you dumped Carmella." His eyes meet mine. "When he found out you were getting married, he snapped. I told him it was a bad idea, but he wouldn't listen to me."

I crack my knuckles, furious that I got his son rather than him. "Your father is an idiot. Carmella cheated on me, so I broke it off. That was years ago now." I shake my head. "My only way to hurt him is to kill you. I don't have time for games. Unless you want to tell me where to find him. Then I'll spare you."

His eyes widen as he stares at me in disbelief. "You want me to rat out my own father?"

I nod. "I want you to make a decision. Tell me

where your father is, and you get to live and take over operations once he's gone. Or you can die now and I'll send your head in a box to him."

Marcus swallows hard, his Adam's apple bobbing as he does. "I'll do it," he says.

Satisfaction sweeps through me. "Perfect. Where will I find him?"

Marcus shakes his head. "He has a base under the Gambini restaurant in the basement. He's been hiding there ever since your wedding."

I smirk at this man's naivety. "Thank you." I turn to walk away.

"Wait, aren't you going to let me go?" he asks.

I stop, shaking my head. "Until I have your father you won't be leaving here." I glance over my shoulder at him. "Sit tight."

I walk out of the cell in the basement of my office block. My phone rings and I dig it out of my pocket, seeing Piero's number flash up. "What is it?" I ask.

"Sir, McCarthy sent a bomb to Aida in a dress box." There's a few moments' pause as my head swims. "She noticed it and took cover before the explosion, but this is an outright act of war."

The relief I feel that she's alive is beyond anything I've ever felt before. It's a sign that I'm starting to get too close to my wife. "Get her checked by Doctor Kingsley. I'm on my way." I cancel the call and walk toward the exit, knowing that my revenge on Donatello will have to wait.

Aida needs me now. I didn't protect her like I promised I would. The guilt is crushing. This is a new sensation. I never care about anyone else, but Aida has infected me like a disease I can't shake.

I PACE THE FLOOR, feeling rage infiltrate every fiber of my being. Aida could have died while I was off torturing Marcus Donatello.

I never feel this out of control. Malachy has declared war by trying to kill my wife. It turns out the coward I killed was his cousin. Malachy wouldn't listen to reason when I told him that his cousin was working for the Russians.

The attempt on Aida's life has me shook when it shouldn't. An arranged marriage should mean she's disposable to me, and when I got the call from Piero, all I felt was panic.

I haven't even gone to see her since the attack, as the doctor confirmed she's fine, just in shock. The thought of facing her makes me feel sick to my stomach, and I can't understand why.

Piero stands in the corner, leaning against the wall. "What's the plan, sir?"

I stop pacing and meet his cool gaze. In the twenty years that I've known the guy, I've never seen anything shake him. Even an attack in my home doesn't seem to rattle his unbreakable resolve. Normally, I'm calm under pressure, but the fact that Malachy struck at my home has messed with my head.

"Malachy must pay for this," I say, running a hand across the back of my neck. "I'm not sure we can avoid war after such a blatant attack." I walk to the dresser at the back of my study and pour myself a glass of scotch. The fiery liquid helps ease the tension coiling through every muscle in my body.

"Do you have any ideas in mind about how to strike back?" Piero asks.

I tip the rest of my glass down my throat before pouring another one. "The Irish run the fucking docks, which is going to be a problem."

Piero clears his throat. "It's a problem I've been thinking about for a while, even before this happened, sir."

I meet his gaze. "Do you have any solutions?"

He nods. "Yes. Salem dock is small, but no one brings their drugs in there. Everyone wants to bring product directly into the heart of the city." He shrugs. "It's ideal if you can bring it straight in, but with a possible war breaking out between the Irish and us, we need to consider alternatives, and I think Salem is perfect."

It's an intriguing idea that might help our bottom line since the Irish don't give us a favorable rate for deliveries or the warehouse we rent at the docks. "How would it work with getting the product into the city?"

Piero looks thankful that I'm considering his idea.

"We buy a few eighteen-wheelers, and we get our guys on the run between Salem and the city. I've spoken to the guy that runs the docks, and he's up for looking the other way." He pulls his cell phone out of his pocket and brings up a price sheet. "Our costs at the dock will be a third of Boston harbor, including rental of a storage unit."

I nod. "Why the fuck didn't you think of this sooner?" It's a joke since it's a genius plan, but Piero clearly thinks I'm serious as he turns as white as a sheet.

"I-I just— "

"Calm down, Piero. I'm messing with you. This is genius."

He relaxes instantly and smiles. "Thanks, sir. Shall I set it up with the dockmaster?"

I nod. "Yes, get the ball rolling as fast as possible." My brow furrows. "Who owns the docks though?"

He shakes his head. "I'm not too sure. Do you want me to check?"

"Yeah. I know Gurin owns a lot of real-estate up in Salem. We don't want to anger the Russians if he owns the docks."

"True. I'll do some digging." He places his cell phone in his pocket and pushes off the wall. "Consider it done."

"Before you go, I have Marcus Donatello in the basement of the offices." I sigh heavily. "He has given up Brando's location. Can you get a few guys to retrieve him?"

"Sure thing, sir. Where is he?"

"The basement of Gambini's. Bring him here so I can deal with him myself."

Piero tilts his head slightly. "What about briefing the guys?"

I hate having meetings with my guys, but unfortunately, the fallout with Malachy makes it necessary. "Set it up for Thursday afternoon but make everyone aware of what has happened. We can't risk anyone getting caught up in any trouble. I need to spend tomorrow with my wife."

Piero nods. "I'll text you the location and time once it's sorted." He walks toward the door and lets himself out of my office, shutting it behind him.

Ever since I lost control after the charity event, I've kept my distance from her. I'm not the kind of man to make a fuss over an attack on my wife, at least not to her face. When Piero called me, I couldn't believe the utter panic that coursed through me when he mentioned a parcel for Aida had exploded.

It irritated me that I felt that panic. I shouldn't care about Aida's wellbeing. But for some reason, I do.

Loosening the tie around my neck, I leave my office and head toward the hallway. There's only one thing left to do, and that's to check on my wife. I've put it off long enough.

The door isn't shut when I get to it. Instead, it's cracked open slightly, and I look into the room. Aida is lying on the bed with her back to me. I can't tell whether she's asleep or not.

I push open the door and walk toward her, setting a hand gently on her shoulder. "Aida?"

She groans and rolls over, opening her beautiful chestnut brown eyes. "Milo?" her voice is raw and hearing her say my name like that drives me wild.

It irritates me how much she affects me.

"How are you doing?" I ask, and it sounds stupid. She was almost blown up, for fuck's sake.

She brushes the hair from her face and sits up. "Tired," she says, not looking me in the eye.

There's been a disconnect between us ever since I fucked her after the charity event. The undeniable sexual tension that had been there from the moment she stepped off that plane has been muted.

"Aida, look at me," I order.

I notice her hesitation as she keeps her eyes fixed to her hands. Irritation coils through me as I wonder if she intends to force me to ask again. Instead, she brings her gaze to meet mine.

There's anger in her eyes—anger so fierce it borders hatred.

Aida hasn't seen the true extent of my darkness. If she thinks my treatment of her has been cruel, she hasn't seen anything yet. I have been kinder to her than any other woman I've met.

"I'm sorry I wasn't here when the bomb exploded." I haven't forgotten my promise I made to her in the ocean outside the grotto, and I meant every word. She may believe I'm a monster, but I protect what is mine. Aida is my property now, whether she likes it or not.

I won't let anything happen to you. I promise. I'll protect you.

My promise hasn't been kept.

She shrugs. "What does it matter? I'm nothing more than a slave to you." Aida looks away from me.

My rage has a life of its own. My possession over this beautiful creature consumes me.

I grab hold of her chin forcefully, pulling her gaze back to mine. "I didn't say you could look away." I search Aida's brown eyes and find the passion of anger inside of them. It mirrors my own.

She spits in my face. "You're a fucking pig," she says.

A growl-like rumble rises from deep in my chest as I let go of her chin and wipe the saliva away. "Have I taught you nothing since you arrived here?" I feel passionate rage infecting my blood.

"All you've taught me is how to hate someone more than I believed humanly possible."

I shake my head, feeling an odd pulling sensation in my chest. "Hate?" I laugh. "Angel, you've hardly seen what I'm capable of."

She swallows hard, and I can see the fear ignite in her eyes. Fear used to be something I relished seeing in a woman's eyes, but not in Aida's. "Oh great, so I can expect to hate you even more."

I grab hold of her wrist hard and pull her close.

"Don't be smart with me. I know how much you love being punished, but you might not like the punishment if you push me any further."

She shakes her head. "Glad to see you're concerned that your wife was almost blown to pieces by your enemy." Aida rips her wrist out of my hand. "Your answer is to punish me for saving my own life as well as Olivia's."

I grit my teeth. Piero had explained what happened. She did save their lives. Otherwise, she would be in critical condition in a hospital, or worse. "No, but spitting in my face and telling me you hate me doesn't help."

Her eyes widen, and she pushes off the bed, putting distance between us. "Don't act like you care what I think about you."

Care.

A word that wasn't in my vocabulary until I met her. I do care what Aida thinks more than I should. I walk toward her slowly. "For some fucked-up reason, I do care." I grab hold of her wrist and pull her into my chest. "Now stop testing me and shut up." I press my lips to hers and kiss her passionately, teasing my tongue around hers.

She tenses at first, reluctant to give into me. However, her resolve slowly waivers as she kisses me back. The pent-up frustration releases as we both devour each other. I lift her in my arms and carry her back to the bed, gently lowering her onto it.

I can't understand why a need to be gentle with her takes hold of me.

Aida looks up at me with a smoldering desire that replaces the hate.

I grab hold of the front of her thin nightdress and rip it in half, making her gasp. The need for her naked and panting beneath me is all-consuming.

I kiss her neck softly, kissing a path slowly down her perfect body. Roughly, I unhook her bra and toss it aside, allowing my tongue to tease around her hard, pebbled nipples.

She moans, her lips pursing in a way that drives me insane. I let my tongue and lips trail down her abdomen toward the apex between her thighs.

Aida is wearing a skimpy little thong that is easy to tear in two with my bare hands.

I bury my face between her thighs, and she makes the most delicious sound I've ever heard. I pause a moment and gaze up at her. "Have you missed daddy's tongue, angel?" I ask.

She bites her bottom lip, nodding. "Yes." She doesn't call me sir or daddy, but I allow it to slide on this occasion.

The hunger for my wife overrules my need to dominate. It drives me insane and is unlike anything I've experienced before in my life. Aida has gotten under my skin. She is so deep-rooted that no matter how much I try to avoid her, I know it'll only come back stronger.

Aida's back arches as I drive my tongue deep inside

of her. All my focus is on turning her into a quivering, begging mess. The need to claim her overwhelms me. I made my intention to get her pregnant clear, but I can't understand why I have a sheer, primal need to mate with the woman I've been tied to who's almost impossible to resist.

When Fabio suggested I marry his daughter, Piero thought it was a good idea as she could provide an heir to my empire and give me control over Alteri's business once he passes away.

However, producing an heir isn't the driving force that makes me want to get her pregnant. It feels like a fundamental instinct that I can't fight. A need to mark her as mine in every physical way possible. The ultimate way of marking her as mine would be to get her pregnant.

I stand behind her and drop my pants and boxer briefs. Without warning, I slide every inch of my cock as deep as possible inside of her. My thrust is gentler than I've been with her up to now. Aida gasps, and it's a sound that sends shock waves through my body. There's something different about this moment together. I'm not sure it's a good thing. It feels unpredictable, and I don't do unpredictable.

21

AIDA

Milo thrust into me with a gentleness that makes my chest ache. For the first time, he's fucking me without punishment. No flogger or paddle in sight. There's a difference in the way he's treating me tonight, and I find it unnerving.

I can't stop his words repeating in my mind like a broken record, as if they mean something. Nothing this man says should matter to me.

For some fucked-up reason, I do care.

If his actions to date are anything to go on, Milo doesn't have the capacity to care for me. Yet, the mere prospect that he could feel something for me makes my insides flutter and my heart race. This twisted and cold-hearted man has managed to worm his way under my skin in ways I can't comprehend.

I feel his hands tightening around my hips as he starts to increase the intensity of his thrusts. It's impossible to keep quiet as he fills me with a pleasure so intense that I crave release more than anything.

"Fuck," Milo growls behind me, digging his fingers into my hips harder. "You feel like fucking heaven," he murmurs.

I groan as he nibbles at the lobe of my ear. I grit my teeth, wishing I had the power to resist him. My hate for him has morphed into something I can't quite describe. A passionate emotion that has blurred as time went on.

Most people get addicted to alcohol or drugs. My addiction is to my husband, despite his cruel treatment of me. It would be easier if I were addicted to anything else.

Milo grabs a handful of my hair and yanks it hard. "I want you to turn over for me, princess."

I turn over onto my back and stare into his ice-blue eyes. Eyes that once scared me because of the lack of emotion they held. But now I can see a depth of emotion that both shocks and excites me. There's a passion in them that boils my blood.

Milo kisses my lips softly as he plunges every inch back inside of me. My stomach churns as I know that his gentleness is only going to confuse me. It's easier to dislike him when he's rough and cruel, but it is impossible to hate him even then. My hunger for the pain he doles out is masochistic.

"Fuck, you're so tight, angel," he murmurs into my ear, thrusting his huge cock in and out of me with long, slow strokes so I can feel every inch of him stretching me.

My nipples harden against his tattooed chest. "Fuck," I mutter.

He wraps a hand around my throat and squeezes enough to hurt. "I want to hear you call me daddy," he orders.

I meet his hot gaze and bite my bottom lip. One minute we're fighting, and the next we're fucking. It's the most messed-up relationship ever.

"Fuck, daddy," I breathe, feeling the need for release tightening its hold over me.

"Good girl," he purrs, making my heart skip a beat.

In all the times we've has sex, he's never allowed me to face him. There's something deeply intimate about it.

Milo is all I've ever known. Sex with him has always been impersonal, but as I look into his eyes, it strips me bare and makes me feel vulnerable. I can see the same vulnerability staring right back at me, as his ice-cold exterior melts away.

His lips tease over mine softly and his neat beard tickles my skin. I feel so insignificant and small as his huge, powerful body covers mine. I'm at my husband's mercy. Milo has the power to break me and my heart. I never should have felt this way about him, but it's as if he stole my heart from right under my nose. A man like him doesn't deserve my care.

"That's it, angel, take daddy's cock," he whispers

against my ear. "I love being inside your perfect, tight pussy."

I shut my eyes, moaning at his dirty words. My nipples are hard peaks as Milo drives me nearer to climax.

He stops, making me whimper in frustration. "I'm going to make you wait, angel. I'm going to keep pushing you to climax, only to stop repeatedly until you're practically begging me to let you come." A cruel glint ignites in his eyes, and for some reason, it turns me on.

Why do I like him treating me like this?

"What?" I ask, trying to push him off me.

He grabs my wrists effortlessly and pushes them down on either side of my head. "I'm in control of your pain, your pleasure." He shakes his head. "I'm in control of you entirely, princess." He uses his body to pin me to the bed as he leans over and grabs a chain already affixed to the bed, clasping my right wrist in the handcuff.

He then grabs another chain, clasps my left wrist in it, and pulls out of me. "I'm going to make you so desperate you'll be crying," he says, towering over me in all his grandeur.

"You're a fucking bastard," I spit, feeling the pain right in the center of my chest. I should have known the gentleness would quickly disappear. Milo is too broken.

His eyes flash with rage, reminding me how angry he got when I called him that before.

He moves like a viper, grabbing my throat so hard I think he's going to choke the life out of me. "Don't call me that again. Do you understand me?" He says each word slowly.

I struggle to swallow with his hand tight around my neck. All I can do is nod.

He lets go of my neck, and I gasp for air. "You're a psychopath," I spit.

"I've been called worse. Don't act like you don't love the way I treat you, Aida." He shakes his head. "I see it in your eyes. How much you long for me."

I glare at him in disbelief, angry at how cocky he is. Although I know deep down that I'm angry at myself because he's right. My body and mind are constantly at war with each other. Milo's cruel, rough touch makes me feel alive. He knows what he wants and he's not afraid to take it, which makes me feel desired in ways I've never experienced before.

His eyes hold a ferocious passion as he watches me, looking feral. Milo's dominant ways are addictive, even if they are so often cruel. No matter what he does, I still crave him.

Milo grabs my ankles, clasping them in the chains fixed to the bed. He then grabs a pole from beneath the four-poster bed.

"What is that?" I ask.

Milo smirks at me—the same smirk that is supposed to intimidate. When we first met, I believed it to be cruel, but now it's an expression that ignites a deep, wanton pulse inside of me. "It's a spreader bar, angel." He tilts his head to the side. "I want you detained and spread wide open for me." He affixes the bar between the two restraints on my ankles.

I watch as he takes a step back and stares at me, taking in the image of me utterly powerless and at his mercy.

"Perfect," he purrs, sending shivers down my spine.

I inhale a deep breath, trying to calm my nerves. My heart pounds at one-hundred miles an hour as I realize I'm at the mercy of a sadist. "What are you going to do to me?"

Milo meets my gaze with his ice-cold blue eyes. "Anything I want."

A shiver starts at the top of my head and runs right down my spine. My eyes remain locked on him as he moves to the nightstand and opens it, searching for something. When he finishes, he's holding a blindfold in one hand and a vibrator in the other.

He doesn't say a word as he places the blindfold over my eyes. A thrilling panic rises inside of me as I can no longer see the predator who has me cornered. There's something uneasy about not being able to see and being tied down, completely at a man's mercy. It makes me feel so weak and insignificant. "Let me go," I shout, wrestling against the restraints as the reality of the situation overpowers me. "I don't like this."

The buzz of the vibrator cuts in, and it feels like my entire body is on fire. Milo presses it against my clit and turns it on high, making my hips rise involuntarily from the bed. "Fuck," I shout.

Milo chuckles a deep laugh that increases the pleasure. There is most certainly something fundamentally wrong with me.

I should hate the man who is enjoying having me at his mercy. Instead, I never want him to stop toying with me. My nipples are hard, painful peaks as Milo adjusts the power of the vibrator, pushing me higher. "Oh my God," I scream, knowing I'm about to tumble over the edge.

At that very moment, Milo turns the vibrator off. "Not yet, angel," he purrs.

I grunt in frustration, shaking my head. "Why are you torturing me?"

He laughs. "If I were torturing you, then you would be in a lot of pain."

"You know what I mean," I say, feeling exasperated by my husband. "Can you at least take this damn blindfold off?"

He growls like a beast, and suddenly I feel his hand around my throat. "You have no say in what happens, Aida. I'm in control. Open your mouth."

I hesitate, which earns me a hard spank on my thigh.

"Now," he orders.

I open my mouth, and suddenly I feel his heavy, hot cock slide to the back of my throat. I gag instantly, but he doesn't stop. All I can do is focus on my breathing and try to use the techniques I googled in the Bahamas.

"That's it, angel. Fuck. Your throat feels like heaven on daddy's cock."

I feel my body responding to his dirty talk and relaxing into the submissive position he has forced me into.

He continues to fuck my throat for a while, leaking salty precum down it. When he finally pulls back, I hear him groan almost in protest. "You're going to learn how good it feels when I deny your release. It is a euphoric feeling."

The buzz of the vibrator makes my thighs quiver in anticipation. Milo presses it against my clit, making me jolt. My body coils from the pleasure Milo is coaxing from me with the device. He's slower this time, starting on a lower setting, which is infuriating. "Oh God," I shout when he has me almost ready to combust.

He turns the device off and leaves me a panting, unsatisfied mess.

"Fuck's sake," I say out of frustration, squirming in my restraints.

Suddenly, Milo's cock slides deep inside of me without warning.

The shock of it makes me tense as every inch of his huge cock slides inside of me. "What the fuck—"

Milo bites my lip, stopping me from saying another word. "All I want to hear coming from your dirty fucking mouth is 'yes, daddy,'" he growls.

It frustrates me how my mind and body obey him on instinct. "Yes, daddy," I cry as he fucks me hard and deep–so deep I don't know where he begins and I end anymore.

He grunts like an animal above me, driving me closer and closer to release. We're both desperate for each other.

"Oh, yes, daddy, I'm going to come," I scream.

Milo chuckles and pulls out of me. "Not yet, angel."

I growl in frustration.

"Or should I say, tiger?" he teases, kissing a path down my neck. "You'll thank me when I let you come."

This tango between us goes on for what feels like an eternity. Milo denies both of us our releases, fucking my pussy and throat repeatedly. He licks me close to climax only to stop at the last minute or uses the vibrator.

By the time he brings me close again, I'm exhausted and almost crying. "Please, daddy. I need to come," I beg, feeling tears welling in my eyes.

His strokes are slow and torturous, driving me insane. "Is that right, angel? Do you think you deserve to come?"

I nod. "Yes, daddy. I've done everything you asked. Please." I sound like a whining little brat, but that's what he's reduced me to. I'm desperate and needy, like a whore.

"Okay, angel. I'm going to fuck you until you come on my cock." He bites my bottom lip before kissing me deeply. His thrusts become faster and harder as he grunts above me. Our bodies meet in a frantic, primal clash of skin on skin.

My hard nipples graze against his muscular chest as he continues to plow in and out of me. Despite my exhaustion, the pleasure is unparalleled. Each time he brings me close to climax, it feels better than the last, promising that he will be true to his word.

"I'm going to breed your little pussy and fill you with so much cum you'll be dripping for hours." He digs his fingertips into my thighs and plows into me harder, the spreader bar keeping me wide open. "I want you to come all over my cock, princess," Milo says.

It feels like my soul leaves my body the moment he pushes me over that edge. Every muscle in my body spasms at the force of my orgasm. I feel a gush of wetness spreading over my thighs.

"Fuck, yes," Milo groans. "Come like a good girl." His voice is deep and husky. For the first time, Milo sounds out of control.

He roars as he comes too, flooding my pussy with his seed. Breeding me the way he promised he would.

It feels like I'm floating on a cloud, no longer aware of anything but the white-hot pleasure that Milo makes me feel. It's a pleasure beyond anything I ever could have imagined. It blows my mind. My vision turns white behind the blindfold, and I wonder if I've died from too much of a good thing.

It takes what feels like a few minutes for me to return to the present. Suddenly, the blindfold is removed, and Milo is already undoing the cuffs around my ankles and removing the spreader bar. A sudden sense of emptiness sweeps over me.

Milo made me feel better than I believed possible, but as he quickly clears up, hardly glancing in my direction, he erases all of that in an instant. Milo will never answer my need for him to hold me the way I long to be held.

Once he unshackles my wrists, he does get under the covers with me. However, my longing to have him hold me goes unanswered as he gently places a hand over mine.

I glance at his face, which is impossible to read. The cold, emotionless look has returned to his eyes. He's bringing down a wall between us after such an intimate moment.

I focus on the warmth of his hand on mine. It makes me feel safe for some reason, even though this man is anything but safe. He's dangerous, and feeling anything but hatred for him gives him too much power over me.

Too bad I think the ship has already sailed. Milo holds my heart in his hands, and he could crush it at any moment.

My eyes flicker open as the sun streams through the bedroom window. The ache between my thighs reminds me of the intimate night I spent with Milo.

I turn over to find his side of the bed empty and cold. He's been up for a while. I rub my hand across my face, groaning. My relationship with my husband is becoming more complicated by the day. Especially since I saw a side of him that makes me wonder if there is something good worth fighting for under all that cruel, cold hatred.

It's an odd feeling, hating a man for ripping away my liberties and commanding me like a slave yet loving the way it feels when he does exactly that, dominating me in a way that empowers me. Milo is almost an animal when we're together, which makes me feel desired in ways I can't explain.

The click of the bathroom door opening draws my attention to it. Milo steps out of the bathroom with a towel loosely hanging around his hips. His dark hair is wet and slicked back. Beads of water roll down his perfectly chiseled chest that is covered in dark ink. He's a picture of perfection.

"Morning, angel," Milo purrs, smiling easily. It's a casual smile that sets my world on fire and my heart fluttering in my chest. "I didn't mean to wake you."

I shake my head, sitting up in bed. "You didn't. I thought you were gone when I woke."

His jaw clenches and his eyes mist with desire as they move lower from my face. It's at that moment I realize the duvet fell and I'm sitting there with nothing on.

I clear my throat and cover myself up, which draws a growl of displeasure from my husband. "I've told you never to cover yourself up." I swallow hard as he approaches the bed. "I thought we could spend the day together," he says.

Those words were the last words I expected to hear. "What do you have in mind?"

He shrugs. "You've hardly seen any of the city. I thought I'd show you around."

I keep my gaze trained on my hands, wishing I didn't have to go anywhere. "Isn't it dangerous after what happened yesterday?"

He kneels on the bed in front of me and grabs my chin, forcing me to look him in the eye. "No one can touch you if you are with me," he says, with so much self-confidence. "No one would dare."

I tilt my head to the side. "How can you be certain of that?"

His jaw clenches, and he looks angry. "I don't like being questioned, Aida. There's no man alive stupid enough to try to take what is mine from me." He shakes his head. "Not while I'm there, at least." He gets off the bed, dropping the towel to the floor.

My stomach somersaults at the sight of him naked. I've seen him naked when we've fucked, but never been allowed to admire his body this close.

He turns, and his cock is as hard as a rock. "Like what you see?"

I feel the heat spreading up my chest and neck,

which is ridiculous considering everything he did to me last night.

There's not a part of my body he hasn't seen from many different angles, and yet I feel vulnerable because he's caught me staring at him the way he stares at me.

Milo may have been cruel since the day we met, but the one thing that's undeniable is the palpable attraction that has always existed between us.

I know I need to escape this man before it's too late. This twisted thing between is turning into something I never wanted it to. I'm at risk of being burned by a man so cruel he wouldn't care if he broke my heart in two. In fact, I fear he would enjoy it. After all, he is a sadist.

Somehow, I need to save myself before there's nothing left to save but a broken, empty shell of my former self.

22

MILO

By the time I get Aida out of the house, it's almost lunchtime. My men are getting a head start on plans to strike back at Malachy for his attack on my wife ahead of tomorrow's meeting. If his attack taught me anything, it's that I've been spending too much time avoiding her.

Aida sits away from me in the back of the town car I asked James to bring around today. It's better for runs into Boston than the limousine, even if it's not as comfortable.

My hands are itching to reach over for hers, but I keep them in my lap. It's been clear since the Bahamas that my attraction to my wife is a dangerous problem.

Aida is already at risk of falling for me, if she hasn't fallen already. It's the reason I kept a distance from her when we returned from the Caribbean.

I clench my jaw as a voice in my head shouts "Liar!"

This trip into Boston was a mistake, but it's a bit late now to change my mind. I have been feeling sensations around Aida that I'm not used to feeling. When Piero rang me and told me about the explosion, I thought only of Aida. I never think about anyone except for myself, normally.

No matter how much I try to tell myself that it's because I'm so vested in the deal with Fabio, I know it's not true. Aida has ignited something inside of me I never knew existed: the capacity to care for another human being.

"What would you like for lunch?" I ask her, breaking the awkward silence that has fallen between us since we got into the car.

She looks at me, and the suspicion in her eyes tells me she thinks it's a trick question. "I thought you were always in control. Why does it matter what I want?"

I sigh heavily. "Aida, I may be in control, but if I ask you what you want for lunch, then I intend to give you the option to choose."

She looks down at her hands, which she fidgets with. "Are there any good Sicilian restaurants in Boston?"

I smile. "Of course. There are a few." It's good that I own the best one in the city. "I own the best one."

Aida raises her eyebrows. "Do you like Sicilian food?"

I laugh. "Of course. I have Sicilian roots too, even if I was born in Boston."

She nods. "Of course. I forget because of your accent."

I do have an American accent, but my Italian is impeccable. My father taught me to speak Italian properly from a young age. "Sei più bella di un angelo," I speak as proof, telling her she's more beautiful than an angel. It's the truth. She is stunning, and I still can't get over how lucky I was to land an arranged marriage to a girl as attractive as her.

She blushes, and it's annoyingly adorable. "Grazie. Anche tu sei bellissimo." She tucks a hair behind her ear.

Her voice is sincere when she calls me beautiful, even though it's laughable. I've never been called beautiful. Handsome, yes, but beautiful is a benevolent word, and I'm anything but.

"What is the name of your restaurant?" she asks, changing the subject.

I smile, knowing she'll like the name of the restaurant. "Palermo."

A sad smile twists on her lips, and she sighs. "I miss Sicily so much. Have you been?"

My brow furrows. "Of course. I was there two months ago when I came to meet your father. We agreed on the deal for your hand in marriage in Palermo."

She swallows. "Oh, I thought your trip to Sicily two months ago was made up when you told everyone at our wedding reception."

I shake my head. "No, it seemed appropriate to use that trip since I missed a charity event while in Sicily with your father." I run a hand through my hair, surprised at how easy conversation can be between us when we're not fighting.

I noticed it on our honeymoon and again now. It's a warning sign I should heed.

I press the intercom and speak to James. "Can we head straight for Palermo, please?"

James responds, "Yes, sir."

I glance at Aida to find she's watching me intently. "What are you looking at, angel?"

She shrugs. "You."

I narrow my eyes. "Why? Do you want me to fuck you in the back of the town car?" I smirk callously. "Believe me. I would."

She shudders and shakes her head. "No, I just..." She trails off, not finishing her sentence, and I'm glad. I don't want to know what was going to come out of her mouth.

"What is your favorite Sicilian dish?" I ask.

She looks a little discouraged but smiles. "That's easy. It has to be arancini. I hope you serve it?"

I nod. "Of course. What kind of Sicilian restaurant would we be without it?"

"A terrible one," she replies, looking thoughtful. "What's your favorite?"

"I do love Arancini, but you can't beat a fresh pasta alla norma."

She nods in agreement. "Well, we know what we are getting then. Arancini followed by pasta alla norma. That's one of my favorites too."

I nod as an oddly comfortable silence falls between us. Weirdly, the comfortable silence only makes me uncomfortable.

Today is not going as I hoped. I can't get out of my head. Aida has gotten under my skin, and I don't know how to get her out since fucking and dominating her isn't working. It's a problem I don't know how to deal with.

"THAT WAS DELICIOUS," Aida says, smiling up at me in a way that makes my heart skip a beat.

I smile back, trying not to let her know how shaken up I am by the feelings rising inside of me whenever she's close.

Controlling every situation is my forte, yet I feel so out of control when I spend time with Aida.

"I'm glad you enjoyed it, angel." I wave Guiseppe over. "Delicious food, Guiseppe. Can I get some cannoli to go, please?"

Aida's face lights up. "I love cannoli too," she says once he leaves to fetch the order.

"Good. I hope the food was to your liking?"

She nods. "It's nice to know I can still enjoy a small

piece of my home." There's a mournfulness in her eyes, and seeing it makes my chest ache.

What is happening to me?

"I miss Sicily so much," she says.

I shrug. "It's nice there for sure, but it's more like a holiday destination than a home."

She shakes her head. "That's because you've never lived there. If you had, you'd feel different."

"I don't know, but you've hardly seen what Boston has to offer yet. Once you do, you may like it here more." I can't understand why I so desperately want to make her feel at home.

"What are you going to show me today?"

The last time I spent any time in Boston without it being for work was so long ago I can hardly remember. When my mother was alive, I loved it when she took me to the public gardens and told me all about the history.

My mother missed Sicily too. I remember her telling me about it, but she used to say that you have to love the home you've been given. Despite my father's inexcusable treatment of her, she somehow had this unwavering positivity. It was infectious, but once she died, it felt like all hope was extinguished from the world with her.

I wasn't allowed to grieve as anytime my father caught me crying, he'd beat me. I often wished he'd beat me hard enough to send me to live with my mother. At that age, I couldn't understand death, but everyone told me she was in a better place. I wondered why she'd left me in a worse place with my father without taking me with her.

"Milo?" Aida asks, placing her hand over mine on the table.

I shake my head. "Sorry. I thought we'd visit the public gardens. They're beautiful in the summer." I force a smile at Aida. "I figured it's the natural beauty you are missing from the islands, so I thought that would be a good place to start."

"Sounds wonderful."

I stand and offer her my hand, which she takes. Just like when we were in the Bahamas, it would be easy for anyone to believe that we were a normal and happily married couple. If only people knew the truth.

James is waiting with the car outside, and I open the door for Aida. "Where would you like to go now, sir?"

"Boston Common and Public Garden."

James nods before lowering the privacy screen as he always does. Aida takes my hand as I sit next to her in the back of the car.

I look down at our entwined hands and feel a mix of panic and happiness. I want to give in to these odd feelings I have for my wife, but I know how dangerous caring for anyone is. Especially when you're the head of one of the most dangerous organized crime groups in North America. It's safer if Aida remains my whore who I do with as I want. If she becomes more to me, then she could be my downfall.

Aida looks like a little kid in a candy store as she walks through the gardens, finding joy in everything she sees. However, being in the gardens makes my chest constrict because of the memories with my mother. Memories that are almost impossible to ignore and somehow seeing Aida's positivity only reminds me of her more.

I struggle to understand how she remains positive after her father sold her to me as part of a business deal.

I never could understand how my mom remained positive after all my father put her through. Aida glances back at me, and her smile wavers. "Are you okay?"

I set my hands on the railing of the bridge. A bridge I came to as a child to feed the ducks with my mother. "It's been a long time since I last came here." I'm surprised to hear myself talking at all, especially admitting that out loud to her.

"Really? Why is that?" Aida asks, looking up at me with wide, innocent eyes.

I remember her telling me about her mother's murder. Aida was only eleven years old, but her mother didn't die because of something Aida did. The guilt I've carried around over my mother's death has almost killed me. I think it's why I'm so dead inside.

If I hadn't broken that vase that day, maybe she'd be alive today. However, I know that's probably not true. My father beat my mother most nights for something, and he likely would have beaten her that night as well. It still doesn't make it any easier.

Aida looks at me patiently and expectantly. All I feel in that moment is a rush of pure adoration for my wife. It's impossible to contain as it floods through me.

"My mother liked to bring me here for picnics and to feed the ducks." I shake my head, swallowing the lump in my throat. "I haven't been here since she died."

Aida sets a hand on my shoulder to console me. All it does is make me panic as I know I shouldn't open up to her or care about her. If you care about people, it can only result in hurt.

I turn away from her to put space between us. Aida takes my hand firmly, pulling me back to her. "Why don't you tell me about her?"

An invitation to open up my heart to the woman who has gotten so deeply under my skin. My head and heart are at war with one another. Our relationship can only end in heartbreak for one or both of us, and yet I still turn to meet her gaze.

23

AIDA

I take Milo's hand, stopping him from walking away. "Why don't you tell me about her?"

His ice-blue eyes hold sadness at the mention of his mother. The careful, emotionless mask he always holds in place is gone, and a vulnerable man stares back. A man that is broken and scarred.

He shakes his head, looking down at our entwined hands. "You're the first person I've spoken to about her since she died."

My brow furrows. That's a long time. "How did your mother die?" I ask, wondering why he wouldn't speak about it to anyone in that amount of time.

His jaw clenches, and his nostrils flare slightly. "My father beat her, and she couldn't recover from her injuries."

My eyes widen in shock. "I'm so sorry—"

"Don't," he growls.

I jump at the sudden change in the tone of his voice. "Don't what?"

He lets go of my hand. His defensive mask slides back into place. "I don't need anyone's pity. It's the reason I don't talk about my mother." He clenches his fists by his side and stares at the water below.

It's crazy the way he changes so suddenly, but he's finally allowed me a glimpse into why he's so defensive. The reason why he's determined to keep me out: fear.

"Milo, I don't want to keep fighting you," I say, hoping that maybe this could be the moment our relationship could blossom into something stronger than I ever believed. "When my father sent me across the Atlantic to meet you, I never expected to feel such a—"

"Stop, Aida." He shakes his head, and there's nothing in his eyes when I meet his gaze. "Don't embarrass yourself. There's nothing more between us. You are my wife who will provide me with an heir."

Pain clutches around my throat and chest. It's so profound it feels like it infects my blood, making every part of my body hurt.

Milo feels what I feel. I know he does. He's just too scared to admit it.

"I told you what your position was, and you should have listened." He shakes his head, his fists clenched. "If you're stupid enough to fall for me after the way I've treated you, then it's your fault."

It hurts as bad as I expected. What little hope I had that Milo had the guts to admit his feelings to me has been extinguished. My stomach churns as I turn away from him to hide the tears flooding down my cheeks. I always knew that my feelings for him were dangerous.

A man as broken as he is can't love, or at least doesn't want to. For the first time, I don't see him as a twisted and cruel man who wants to hurt me. I see him as that seven-year-old boy too scared to love again after his father took his mother from him.

All I know is I can't take this any longer. I won't let Milo break my heart repeatedly. Milo has closed himself off from love, and I won't wait around for him to open his heart to me.

EVER SINCE OUR moment together in the gardens in Boston, Milo has been avoiding me. The moment where it felt like everything shifted between us, if only for a few seconds. When he stared at me and held my hand, the look in his eyes was one of pure adoration.

His coldness had melted away entirely for a brief time. He revealed the real man behind the monster, but he retreated behind his mask at the flip of a switch.

It's been a week since that day, and he hasn't touched me since.

Every day, he leaves early in the morning and doesn't come to bed until late at night. I'm going out of my mind with boredom. This house is a prison, and I've got nothing to do. Over the past three days, I've turned my attention to escape plans, and I'm sure I have the ideal one.

Today, I'm getting myself out of this hell. I don't know what I'll do once I'm out, but it can't be too hard to find a plane to Sicily. At least, I hope it's not. I'm out of touch with how the world works. My father has a private jet, and it's the only way I've ever traveled.

The longing to be back in Palermo is too strong to deny anymore. Milo is insufferable. Every time I think that maybe there could be hope for something real between us, he pulls away. His heart is frozen over, and I don't have the heat to thaw it.

My plan to get out of this house is genius. The guards work in rotations, and I've been so bored the past few days that I've studied them. The guard at the front door leaves to switch with the guard at the back at eleven o'clock every morning. He then goes to fetch him and they have a cigarette together.

It leaves three minutes for me to dash out the door and make it to the cover of the trees near the front of Milo's home. I can make it out of the holes in the broken fencing at the front of his home. It should go without a hitch. And from there, I need to rely on public transport to get me to the airport.

I check my watch and see that it's five minutes to eleven. Milo isn't discreet about where he keeps the cash. There's a safe in our closet. I managed to see him input the code when we were both in there together.

I have five-thousand dollars, which should be

enough to get me to Sicily, I hope. My passport is packed in my rucksack. There's no way that Milo will catch me before I can hop on a plane and get away from him forever.

I lean against the wall, waiting patiently for the guard to leave his post. Like clockwork, he leaves at the stroke of eleven o'clock. I smile as I glance around, making sure no one is around, before making my exit.

My escape is going to be easier than I ever imagined. This entire time I've thought there was no way out and that I was resigned to my fate, and yet the answer to freedom has been staring me in the face the entire time.

I slip out of the front door and check that there are no guards around to catch me. After a few seconds, I'm certain it's clear. With my hood up and my black coat wrapped tightly around me, I sprint for the cover of the trees.

My heart is pounding so fast and hard it feels like it might beat right out of my chest. Once I make it to the trees, I move more slowly against the back fence. When we drove in here yesterday afternoon, I noticed a few holes in the panels big enough for me to squeeze through.

I come to the first one and shrug my backpack off first, placing it to one side. It's going to be a tight squeeze, but I should get through. After carefully contorting myself using my rusty gymnastics skills from high school, I manage to get through. I grab my backpack from the other side and shrug it back onto my shoulders before quickly checking that no one saw me.

It's clear of any guards, and I slowly walk down the sidewalk with my hood up, making sure I don't arouse suspicion by walking too fast. I'm so close to getting away that I can almost taste it.

My heart skips a beat when I see a black town car drive past. It doesn't slow until it gets to the gates.

Out of intrigue, I turn and glance to see that the back is empty. Milo isn't in the car.

I can't understand why my stomach sinks when I don't get one last glance at my husband, a man who has been nothing but cruel to me since the day we met. It's pathetic how much I long for him to feel the way I do.

Adjusting the backpack on my back, I continue to march in the direction of the bus station. It may have been easier to call a cab, but I turned my phone off when I left the building. Milo isn't stupid, and I know he would have ways of tracking me through my cell phone. The best choice is to take the less likely route to avoid getting caught.

When I get to the bus stop, the bus is already there waiting. I can hardly believe my luck as I pay for my fare and sit at the back of the bus, looking out of the window.

A couple of rough-looking guys get on after me, sitting closer than I'm comfortable with.

"This is going to be one fun trip, ain't it, lad?" one of them says, glancing back at me briefly.

My stomach twists as I recognize their accents. They're Irish, and I know the man who attempted to blow me to pieces in Milo's dining room was Irish. It's stupid to paint them all with the same brush. These guys probably have nothing to do with Malachy McCarthy, Milo's enemy who I've heard far too much about lately.

I hug my jacket tighter around me and keep my focus on the sidewalk, rushing past the window. My heart is hammering at a thousand miles an hour.

It's a forty-minute bus ride to the airport, and although the Irish men are still on the bus, they've barely looked at me since. I'm thankful, though, when I get off the bus and head for the terminal building ahead.

All that relief escapes me when I hear a voice behind me. "Where are you going to then, lass?"

The Irish guy that had glanced at me on the bus is standing too close to me. I turn around and find him and his two friends looming over me threateningly.

I shake my head. "I don't want any trouble. Please don—"

One of the other guys interrupts me, "Unfortunately, you have trouble because of your husband."

My muscles tense at the mention of Milo. "I think you've got the wrong person. I'm not married."

The guy at the front laughs. "Sorry, lass, you can't play that game with us. We watched you creep out of his home. You're Aida Mazzeo, and you're coming with us." He reaches for me, and I start backward before breaking into a sprint away from them.

The terminal building is only two-hundred meters away. If I can get inside, then people won't stand by while a woman is being assaulted. I pour all my strength and energy into reaching the building.

I can hear their footsteps thudding on the concrete behind me, getting closer and closer.

"You can't run from us, lass," one of them shouts.

I grind my teeth together as my calves burn. It's been a long while since I've run that fast. When I make it to the terminal building entrance, I'm surprised that they haven't already caught me.

A woman gasps in surprise as I almost knock her over, running into the building. I glance around the lobby, which is packed with people, wondering where to go to find out about getting to Sicily. A sign for the information desk catches my eye, and I rush through the crowd toward it.

Once almost at the desk, I glance back to check for the men that chased me in here. Thankfully, I don't see either of them. "Hello. Can I help you, miss?"

I nod and pull out my purse. "Yes, I want to find out how to get to Sicily from here."

The man's eyes widen. "We don't have any direct flights to Sicily." He types on his computer for a moment. "Your best option is to take the flight to Rome. Then from Rome, I'm sure you can make it to Sicily."

I sigh a breath of relief, thankful that there is a

direct flight from Boston to Italy at all. The quicker I get out of this country, the better. "That would be perfect. Can I buy a ticket from you?"

The guy shakes his head. "No, you need to buy it from the Alitalia desk." He points over at another counter. "There's a flight in three hours to Rome."

I smile. "Great. Thank you for your help."

He nods. "No problem."

I turn around and collide with someone. My stomach sinks as I look up at the man that had chased me from the bus. I feel woozy and realize that he's drugged me.

Reaching forward, I try to fight against him. Instead, he grabs hold of me and yanks me further away from the desk. My jaw feels heavy as I try to speak, but all my words come out slurred, as if I'm drunk. Whatever drug he's administered doesn't knock me out, but it makes me feel like I'm no longer in control of my body. It feels like I'm a doll that he can do whatever he wants with.

"Come on, lass, let's get you home to Malachy."

My stomach churns at the mention of the man who tried to kill me. I can't believe that I could have been on my way back to my home country in three hours. Instead, I'm being dragged into a feud between two megalomaniacs who don't care about anyone but themselves. Malachy is bound to be as messed up as my husband is.

24

MILO

I circle Brando Donatello, knowing that this piece of shit barely warrants my time. Yet, his disrespectful attack on my wedding is proof enough that I need to end his life.

Carmella has been impossible to track down. I'd hoped to find her and torture her along with her pathetic excuse of a father. "Where is your daughter?" I ask again, holding the tip of the knife I'd stabbed into his thigh against his throat.

He spits at me. "You know where she is, you bastard. She's been missing for three weeks now. I know you are behind it." The hate in his eyes indicates that he's not lying. He truly believes I have Carmella.

I shake my head. "Unfortunately, I don't have your daughter. Although, I hope someone crueler than me does." I crouch down so that I'm at eye level with him. "I still have your son, though. Marcus."

A flash of panic enters his eyes. "You are bluffing."

I smirk at that and stand, nodding at Piero to bring his son in. "I never bluff, Brando. You should know that by now."

Piero drags his beaten son into the room and brings him over to us, dropping him in front of Brando.

"Here is your proof."

Marcus glares at me through his busted eye. "You told me you'd let me go."

I nod. "Yes, and I'm a man of my word." I clench my jaw and cut the ropes binding Marcus. "You are free to go, but maybe first you should tell your father why I'm letting you go."

Marcus tenses. "I think you've done enough damage, Mazzeo."

I shake my head. "I beg to differ. I told you that you would be set free, but only one of you is getting out of here alive." I step toward Brando and cut his bindings. "Your son gave us your whereabouts. Now you need to decide which of you dies."

Piero nods in signal and I chuck the knife at a good distance from both.

"May the best man win." I turn around and head out after Piero, who locks the door behind him.

"That was cold, sir."

I glare at my second in command. "What did you expect after the two of them disrespected me?"

Piero shrugs. "Nothing less, sir. The men are waiting

in the boardroom for you." His eyes move to my blood-stained hands. "It may be best to wash up before."

I nod. "I'll see you up there."

The bathroom is empty as I open the door and stand in front of the sink, running the water until it's warm. I watch as the blood stains it crimson. When I glance up in the mirror, I can hardly recognize myself anymore. Blood and violence are all I know. It's not something that used to shock me, but ever since I met Aida, I'm becoming soft.

I finish washing the blood from my hands and grab a paper towel, drying them. After one last look at the shell of a man staring back at me, I head to the boardroom.

My six lieutenants watch me as I enter. Even here in my element I'm not totally focused. Aida consumes every one of my waking thoughts and it's a distraction I don't need when I'm at war with the Irish.

Malachy won't see sense. After an attempt to reconcile our differences, it appears that murdering his cousin made this an impossibility. There's no ground to move on either side, and the man I haven't yet killed seems to be unimportant to him. He even said, *"Kill the fucking bastard. I don't give a shit."*

"Sir, what is the plan?" Piero asks, prompting me to speak.

We're at a stalemate. The only option is war, and it's going to get bloody. "There's nothing left to do but go to war," I reply, walking to the head of the table and taking my seat.

All my men nod in agreement. "Yes, but do we intend to retaliate for Malachy's attempt to murder your wife?"

I wronged Malachy by killing one of his family members. His men weren't acting under his orders when they stole my shipping container of cocaine, so it's not his responsibility. He struck back by trying to take my wife from me. "We must respond with an equally aggressive attack, but who matters to Malachy McCarthy?"

Silence falls over the boardroom as Malachy is more private than I am. He doesn't let anyone from the outside know who he's close to. None of my men knew that man we captured was his cousin. Otherwise, we may have thought twice before killing him.

"We don't know anything about the guy. Shall we torture it out of our friend?" Piero asks.

I tilt my head, considering torturing our captive as an option. The man he's talking about is strong—too strong to give up information that sensitive. He's as loyal as they come. "It would be futile to waste time on him." I wave my hand. "We'll keep him as a possible bargaining chip later on, but that man won't betray Malachy."

Angelo is the next to speak, "What do you propose, sir?"

I have been thinking about how to get back at

Malachy. The only option is to take something I know he loves. It's not a person, though. His 1967 L88 Corvette Convertible is his pride and joy. If I can't take away someone he cares about, I'll get the next best thing. "The corvette. Blow it up."

Orfeo nods, smirking. "Fucking good idea, boss."

I'm not too fond of Orfeo. He's a hothead who likes blowing things up a little too much, but he was the best I had to take over from Sandro after he died. Out of all my lieutenants, he is the only one I don't fully trust. "Get it done. We will see how he reacts, but ensure all your men are briefed before we act." I stand buttoning my suit jacket. "Everyone needs to be on alert to the danger Malachy poses."

All my men stand too. "Yes, sir," they respond in unison.

I run a hand through my hair, letting out a shaky breath. Malachy's attack has me rattled, which is a first for me. He tried to take my wife, which shouldn't matter, but it matters more than I can comprehend.

Aida has managed to mesmerize me. In Boston Public Gardens, there was a moment between us—a moment that frightened me away. Piero clears his throat from behind me. "Are you happy for me to leave Orfeo in charge of the Corvette?" he asks.

I nod. "It's probably the only thing I can trust Orfeo to do: blow something up."

Piero laughs at that. "Yeah, I guess you're right."

He pats me on the shoulder before leaving me alone

in my boardroom. There's a lot at stake if we lose this war to Malachy. Wars between criminal gangs always end with one or the other bowing out and giving over a part of their empire as a truce. Although, there have been wars that continue for years in other cities with no way of finding common ground.

All I can do is hope that this won't be a long war. We have more power than the Irish in this city, but they are renowned for being stubborn bastards. If this is a long-term war, we'll be looking over our shoulders for a long time. Too many casualties come from war, and it almost always gets personal. I always prided myself on having nothing to lose, but now I have everything to lose.

My angel—Aida.

THE MOMENT JAMES pulls the car into the drive, I know something is wrong. All the guards are assembled at the front of the house. Olivia is gesturing at them angrily.

"What the fuck has happened?" I mutter.

James shakes his head. "I don't know, sir. Would you like me to find out before you enter the house?"

I shake my head. "No, let me out here."

He comes to a stop right in front of the crowd of staff. They're so busy shouting at each other they don't even notice me.

"What the fuck is going on here?" I ask, raising my voice loud enough to stop everyone in their tracks.

Everyone turns to look at me with wide, panic-stricken eyes. Something is wrong. Olivia is the one to approach me. "I have some bad news, sir." She swallows hard. "Aida isn't in her room, and we can't find her anywhere in the house."

"What?" I question calmly, wondering if I heard that right.

Olivia glances at one of my guards, and he steps forward. "It was my fault, sir. We believe she may have left the house when I went to change posts on my watch."

White-hot panic slams into me at first. "How the fuck did Aida get out when I have ten guards on patrol at all times?" I growl.

The guard shakes his head in response. "We've searched the grounds but haven't found her yet. Do you want us to widen the search outside the grounds?"

Idiot.

My panic quickly morphs into a rage. I turn away from the guard for a moment, pulling free the knot of my tie. "Cazzo," I growl, turning back and punching the guard in the face.

The rest of the household staff gasp. The crack of the guard's nose breaking is a satisfying sound. My rage has a life of its own as I grab hold of his collar. "You piece of shit. You have one job: to guard my home and keep my wife safe." I punch him in the face again, hard enough to make him bleed. "I should kill you for this."

"Sir, wait," Piero says from behind me, rushing up to the scene. He sets a firm hand on my shoulder. "Breathe, sir. Let's go inside."

I spin around, ready to attack Piero.

He stands in front of me with his shoulders squared, ready to receive the force of my rage. Piero is fearless as he stares me in the eyes. "If you need to hit someone, then hit me." He shrugs. "It won't help find your wife, though."

As always, my capo is my voice of reason. I inhale a long, slow breath to calm myself down. I turn to face my staff. "I want her found, or there will be hell to pay. Do you hear me?"

I'm met with everyone nodding frantically in response. I clap my hands. "Well, get on with it then," I growl.

Everyone rushes away from me, except for the guard that fucked up. He admitted it was his fault, but I've never lost control like that in front of my staff. Everyone knows who I am and what I'm capable of, but they also always witness a man in control.

When they told me that Aida was gone, I snapped. First, I wasn't here when my enemy delivered a bomb into her hands, and now she's escaped.

Piero clears his throat. "Let's get inside and make a plan to find your wife, sir."

I nod, stepping around the broken guard on the

floor. "Yes." I turn my attention to Olivia. "Olivia, can you get someone to sort him out?" I nod toward the guard whose name I don't know.

"Right away, sir."

I walk swiftly into my home, trying to control the rage and panic mixing inside of me. My wife wasn't supposed to be a weapon that my enemies could use against me. Aida was supposed to be nothing more than a means to an end. She gave me a way to get my hands on her father's Sicilian empire once he dies by providing me with an heir to that empire.

Instead, she's become the single most important thing to me in this world. I can't lose her no matter how cruel she thinks I am. No matter how much she hates me for forcing her to stay, I won't let her run. I'll follow her to the ends of the earth. She's mine and always will be.

Piero follows me into my office, where he shuts the door. "Boss, you need to get a handle of your emotions before they eat you alive."

I release a shaky breath, trying to find some sense of control inside of myself. "I can't lose Aida," I reply.

Piero clears his throat. "I take it that your wife has become important to you since you married."

I spin around to face my second in command. "Not a word of this to anyone, do you understand?" I say, glaring at him. There's no way I want anyone other than him to know the true extent of my feelings for the woman I'm wed to.

It looks like it took losing her to admit that even to myself. All I've done is hurt her. The way she looked at me on the bridge in Boston Public Garden cut me to the core, but I coated my heart in steel. I didn't let her in. I couldn't. The last thing I want is to feel the pain I felt when my father murdered my mother.

I'm a fool, since pushing her away has only put her in danger. We're at war with the Irish, and Aida has run away. She's alone in Boston with no clue about this city.

"Your secret is safe with me, sir."

I nod in reply. "They had better find Aida. It's not safe for her on the streets with the war between the McCarthy clan about to start."

Piero's brow furrows. "Do you think we should put a hold on blowing up the Corvette until we recover her?"

I clench my jaw, knowing that giving that order would look weak. If I delay my attack because my wife has gone missing, my men will think I've lost the plot. It's not an option. If we're going to war, I need my men to be able to trust my judgment. "No, we go ahead with the plan as agreed."

All I can do is hope that Aida keeps as far away as possible from any of the McCarthy clan. Malachy wouldn't be merciful if he got his hands on her. After all, he tried to blow her to pieces in my own home. I can't even think about what he'd do if he could get his hands on her.

25

AIDA

The soothing sound of water cresting filters through the air. For a moment, I'm lying on the beach in Sicily, listening to the waves crashing against the shore gently.

When I open my eyes, the reality couldn't be farther from the beach in Sicily. I'm tied to an old wooden chair in the center of a warehouse full to the brim with cocaine. I know what tons of cocaine look like since my father takes shipments regularly in Sicily. He supplies most of the cocaine consumed in Italy and a huge amount of Europe.

It's hard to believe that the Irish and the Italians supply the stuff here, fighting against each other to sell.

A flood of panic twists at my gut when I see three men walk past with machine guns, patrolling the floor.

I shut my eyes, hoping that no one noticed I was awake. The last thing I want is to be tortured into telling them things I don't even know. If they captured me because they want information then they are going to be disappointed. Milo hasn't told me anything about his operations. I don't even know where he runs everything from.

I hear someone clapping from behind me. "Unfortunately, lass, I know you're awake." I swallow hard, wondering if it's the guy who caught me at the airport. When he walks into view, I realize he isn't one of the men that chased me.

He has short brown hair and a long brown beard, neatly trimmed and well kept. He is wearing a crisp white shirt and a pair of black pants.

"Who are you?" I ask, even though I think I know the answer.

He smirks at me. "Malachy McCarthy, lass. I'm sure you've heard of me."

I nod in response, feeling my stomach sinking further than I believed possible. "Yes, I have."

His smirk is almost manic, and it makes his good looks unappealing. "Good." He rubs his hands together. "I wonder how much you've heard about me."

I swallow hard, wishing I did know the kind of man I was dealing with. In Sicily, everyone heard of Milo because of his family's links with Palermo, but no one has heard of Malachy McCarthy. The look in his eyes suggests he's not sound of mind. He looks insane.

"Only your name," I respond.

He looks excited by the fact that I know nothing

about him. "Oh good. I do love surprises." He walks in a circle around me like a wolf sizing up his prey.

"What do you want?"

He chuckles as he circles back, standing in front of me. "Nothing from you, other than silence." His eyes narrow. "How did you end up married to Milo, anyway?"

I grit my teeth and keep silent. This man has captured me, so I'm not sure why he'd want to know anything about our relationship.

"Now you've lost your voice?"

I shrug. "You said you want nothing from me but silence."

He moves closer, leaning over me. "Unless I ask you a question. I get the feeling we aren't going to get on too well, Mrs. Mazzeo."

I hold my chin up high and look him in the eye. The last thing I want to do is show fear.

"I love the ones that come to me with hope. I love breaking it." He slides his hand into his pocket and pulls out a razor blade, flipping it open.

It looks like the situation has quickly taken a dark twist. I can't say I'm surprised.

Malachy twirls the razor blade in front of me. "Do you expect your husband to come and save you, lass?" he asks, delight dancing in his emerald green eyes.

I shake my head. "No, I mean nothing to him." I hate the sinking feeling in my stomach at admitting that. I hate that I care what Milo thinks at all.

Malachy's smile drops. "Shame, that. Is that why you tried to run back to Italy?"

I swallow hard, knowing that antagonizing this guy will result in pain. "Yes, I was trying to escape and go home."

Malachy tilts his head slightly. "Is Milo as much of a bastard as I am when it comes to women, I wonder?" He walks closer to me and places the tip of the blade under my chin, using it to lift my head. "Maybe the two of us should experiment and see, heh?" He licks his lip. "You're a beauty, lass."

Fear takes hold of me at the thought of this man touching me. Milo is the only man I've ever been with, and the thought of any other man makes me sick to my stomach. Especially as I know this maniac would rape me without a second thought. I can see it in his crazed expression. He doesn't care about right or wrong. "I don't think that is necessary. He's a bastard to me. Let's leave it at that."

Malachy laughs. "Do you think you have any say over what happens to you here?" He shakes his head, circling me. The cold metal of the razor blade lands on my shoulder. "I wonder what your pain threshold is."

I shudder in anticipation of this man cutting me to pieces. There's no doubt in my mind that he could murder me horrifically. The look in his eyes tells me he enjoys this too much.

"Where should I cut your pretty skin first?" he muses before pressing down hard into my shoulder and dragging the blade through my flesh. I cry out, unable to hold it in. The pain is unlike anything I've felt before. Blood gushes down my shoulder and onto the shirt I'm wearing, soaking it a crimson red.

Malachy stands in front of me, looking like an excited kid on Christmas morning, ready to open all his gifts. The only thing is, I'm the gift he wants to open with a razor blade.

I clench my jaw, trying to be brave as I stare at my captor. The last thing I need to do is give him the satisfaction of seeing how scared I am on the inside. I'm terrified, but I won't let him know that. My father always warned me about situations like this, but with Aldo following me around all the time, I never believed it would happen.

I should have been more careful without my bodyguard, but I was a fool. Running from Milo has landed me into the claws of a man far worse than him.

He grabs hold of my other shoulder and brings the razor against my throat, cutting the skin. "I bet you wish you didn't try to run from your husband now, don't you lass?" He smells of whiskey as he towers over me. "By the looks of your perfect, creamy skin, he hasn't been nearly as rough with you as he should have been." He brings his face closer to mine. "He's too soft on you. If you had been mine, you wouldn't have run."

Everything that comes out of this man's mouth is laced with a threat, making my stomach churn.

He moves the razor to my collarbone and slices the

skin there. It's excruciating as he drags the blade slowly. I scream, unable to hold back.

Malachy releases me, smirking as he stands with my blood dripping from his razor blade onto the floor. He looks like he's from a horror movie. Again, he's an attractive man but rotten on the inside, a bit like Milo. Although, I know Milo is just damaged. God knows what is wrong with this man.

He circles me again, holding the bloody razor. "I think I need your clothes off so I can survey my options better."

Cold dread slides through my veins at the thought of being naked in front of this man. He uses the blade to cut open my shirt, tearing it off with his hands.

I swallow hard at the disgusting, vicious look in his eyes. "You're a pretty lass. I can see why Milo hasn't ruined you yet." He slides the razor under the right strap of my bra and cuts it free before doing the same on the other. It stays in place until he cuts the main strap around my chest.

Malachy looks at my breasts for a long moment, making me uncomfortable. "I am going to enjoy breaking you." He places the razor just under my breasts and cuts a line in my skin, making me scream.

I feel woozy at the sight of blood, certain I'm going to pass out any moment.

This asshole notices the signs as he grabs hold of my chin forcefully, digging his nails into my face. "Don't blackout on me, lass." He shakes me enough to stop me from fainting. "The fun has barely begun." He steps back, twirling the knife in front of my face.

I swallow hard, knowing that if he cuts me much more, I won't be able to stay conscious.

It's a horrifying thought, that I could pass out and have no idea what this psychopath is doing to me.

Suddenly, someone grabs Malachy's shoulder and pulls him back.

Relief beyond anything I've ever felt floods me as I see Milo punch Malachy in the face. He came for me. I hate how butterflies flutter to life in my stomach.

The hope that perhaps Milo does feel something between us ignites again. It's pathetic how desperate I am to be loved by a man that treated me so cruelly.

26

MILO

Twenty minutes earlier...

"You better have good news for me, Angelo," I say, answering my cell phone.

There are a few moments of silence on the other end. "I've got some good news and some bad news."

I grit my teeth. "Bad first."

Angelo clears his throat. "Malachy is claiming to have Aida."

It feels like my entire world is ripped out from under my feet. Suddenly, I'm spiraling. "Put a stop to Orfeo's plan instantly," I order, knowing that if we blow up Malachy McCarthy's beloved car, he'll do much worse than I can ever fathom to my wife.

Angelo is silent. "That brings me to the good news, although perhaps it will be bad news to you. Orfeo has already successfully destroyed the Corvette."

"Cazzo," I growl, throwing my cell phone at the wall.

It smashes into pieces. Piero clears his throat. "What is it, sir?"

I pace the length of my office without answering. Aida will be dead if I can't get to her fast. Our timing couldn't have been worse. "Malachy has Aida."

"Fuck," Piero says, running a hand through his short hair.

Malachy thinks he's taken my possession that doesn't mean much to me. The move makes me look weak, as though I can't protect my property. Little does he know that he's holding the only thing in this world that I care about.

"Where do you think he will be holding her?" Piero asks.

I think about the question for a few moments, knowing my answer may sound obvious, but I know Malachy. He would select the most obvious place, knowing that we'd never suspect that's where she'd be.

"The docks. I'm sure of it."

Piero's brow furrows. "You think he'd keep her somewhere that obvious?"

I smile at my capo, knowing he's got a lot to learn about the McCarthy clan's leader. "That's exactly the reason she will be there. Get together a team of four of our best men to accompany us to the docks." I crack my neck. "We're going to hit them hard right where it hurts. By the time I'm through with this Irish bastard, he'll wish he never touched her."

Piero's eyes light up, and he nods. "On it, sir."

I watch him as he gets out his cell phone to arrange the team.

My father was an asshole, but the last time war erupted, he was in charge. Although, that war wasn't with the Irish, it was with the Russians. He taught me a lesson: a leader should never step onto the battlefield of war. We should always hide behind our soldiers.

I didn't agree with the sentiment at the time, but this is the first time I've been faced with war since taking over eight years ago. There's no way in hell that I'm sitting back and letting someone else save my wife. I'm the one who must rescue her from Malachy and start making amends for hurting her every time she tries to get close to me. Hopefully, those bridges haven't burned as for some crazy reason I care whether or not she hates me. Aida is mine and always will be.

Piero finishes the call. "Angelo, Tore, Pietro, and Ramon are on their way, sir. ETA ten minutes." He glances at my desk. "Shall we work out a strategy before they arrive and study the map of the docks?"

I nod in response and sit down on the opposite side of the desk. "There are three places Malachy could keep her."

I point at the main port warehouse that the Irish use to bring in their drugs.

Piero runs a hand through his hair. "Fuck, that would be fun."

"Yeah. It's heavily guarded. That's why I think Malachy would hold her there." I crack my knuckles. "Malachy was used to working against my father, but he hasn't had many run-ins with me."

Piero nods. "You two think differently. I don't wish to disrespect your father as he was a great leader, but you have the brains, sir."

He's right. My father was all brawn. His answer to everything was to attack first and think later. Hopefully, Malachy is underestimating my capacity to think how he thinks—to put myself in his shoes.

"Where are the other two places?" Piero asks.

I point at a small building on the shipyard in Boston. "This would be my second port of call, although I'm pretty confident she'll be in their main warehouse."

Piero sighs. "It would be easier if she were in the shipyard."

I nod. "If Aida is not at either of these locations, then they will be holding Aida in the hotel Malachy owns at the docks."

Piero nods in agreement. "Let's hope it doesn't come to that. His hotel is like a fortress, and they have facial recognition CCTV installed." He shakes his head. "We wouldn't stand a chance."

"I agree. Can you get James to bring the SUV around?" I ask.

Piero stands. "Yes, sir. I'll come back for you once everyone has arrived."

I don't say anything as my capo leaves me alone in my office. The bottle of scotch on my dresser is calling to me, but I don't pour myself a glass. If I'm going to pull this off, I need my mind clear.

Aida is counting on me, and I've let her down too many times already by pushing her away. I won't let her down this time.

THE DOCKS ARE CRAWLING with more Irish than I can count. Malachy has increased the warehouse's security, which is expected during a war, but it also suggests that Aida is inside.

Not to mention, Malachy is here too. His Chevy Impala is parked in front of the building.

"We didn't bank on Malachy being here, sir. How are we going to proceed?" Tore asks.

I watch as more Irish enter the warehouse. "It won't change anything." I run a hand across the back of my neck. "I'm glad the bastard is here."

"We must work as fast as possible. The sole intention is to recover Aida and get out."

Piero clears his throat. "I worry that six of us are going to stand out. Maybe two would be a better idea?"

I consider Piero's suggestion. He's right that six of us marching in there would stand out more than two, but if things go wrong, we're going to need backup. It's a vital decision to make as we only get one shot at this.

"Compromise. I'll go in first, followed by Piero and then Tore. The other three will wait outside in the car, but on the radio in case we need backup."

Piero nods in agreement. "I think that's safer, sir."

"Give it two minutes before following, and Tore, two minutes after Piero. It's the best way not to raise suspicion."

Angelo clears his throat. "All due respect, sir, but don't you think you'll be the most recognizable of all of us?"

I glance at my lieutenant. "Possibly, but I won't leave the rescue of my wife to another man."

Angelo nods. "Fair enough. Good luck, sir."

I get out of the car and pull the hood of my jacket over my head. The CCTV cameras are everywhere, but we found a blind spot to park the car.

Slowly, I walk toward the entrance of the warehouse without being spotted. There are so many Irish hanging around. I doubt they'd expect an attack to come from one man in a hooded jacket. That's why this is the perfect plan.

A guy nods at me as I walk through into the warehouse, and I nod back. The adrenaline racing through my veins makes me shake, but I stuff my hands in my pockets and walk through the warehouse.

A few of Malachy's men know what I look like because of our meetings, but they would only be his higher-ranking men. I have to hope I can find Aida before Malachy spots me.

I walk against the wall of the warehouse, keeping in the shadows. The door opens at the far end, and I glance back to spot Piero entering. No one seems to bat an eye at him as he walks into the warehouse, taking the opposite route to me.

Malachy has so many men in his clan that they can't all know each other.

A shrill scream from the back of the building catches my attention.

Aida.

I quicken my pace in desperation to get to her. The warehouse opens into a large room at the back, and I see Malachy standing with his back to me, looming over my wife.

Rage slams into me when I see the razor in his hand coated in her blood. Then I notice Aida is naked from the waist up, and all rational thoughts fly out the window. I don't think about my next move. Instead, I act on instinct to protect what is mine.

Malachy doesn't sense me coming as I grab his shoulder and pull him away from her, punching him hard in the nose.

"Bloody bastard," he shouts, trying to bring a hand up to his nose.

Before he can reach it, I close my hand around his and squeeze so hard he growls. "You take what is mine and don't expect me to come for it, Malachy?" I ask, glaring into the eyes of the sadistic bastard that cut my wife.

He laughs, and that manic look in his eyes sends chills down my spine. We're trying to go to war with a psychopath, which will never end well. I thought I was fucked up, but Malachy McCarthy is crazier than me.

"Aye. You expect to blow up my favorite fucking car and get away with it?" he asks, jumping to his feet faster than I can react.

He comes at me like a viper. His fist connects with my jaw. I shake it off, stepping back to put distance between us.

"You must care for this bitch to come for her yourself," Malachy spits, trying to wind me up.

I won't let him get under my skin. Facing off against him like this isn't ideal, especially after what happened last time we fought.

Malachy McCarthy is the undisputed bare-knuckle champion of Boston. No one can defeat him, and I don't like my chances of trying to beat him in a fight. I've tried before, and it didn't end well. He's a savage and even bit a guy's ear off one time during a street fight.

Maybe I didn't plan this out well, but Piero or Tore can back me up if the fight goes south for me.

Malachy smirks at me as he wipes the blood from his nose. "This is going to be a fun fucking fight, lad."

I shake my head. "Not a fair one considering your experience."

He laughs at that. "All is fair in war. I don't give two shits if it's not fair. I'm going to beat you so bad that you'll be on the brink of death, and then I'll take your beautiful wife and fuck her in front of you."

Fierce rage slams into me. I run toward the Irish son of a bitch, growling as I put all my strength into attacking him. I've never wanted to kill a man more than I want to kill Malachy. I tackle him to the floor and punch him in the face over and over.

He laughs as if he doesn't feel the pain. "That's it, pretty boy. Take out your rage while you have a chance. I'm going to fuck you up." He spits blood into my eyes, and I have to stop to wipe it out.

We will kill each other at this rate. Normally, I don't fight with my fists. Malachy punches me in the jaw again, and it feels like he almost broke it.

I notice Piero creeping into the room behind us, and I hope he plans to get my wife out of here. I didn't think about an exit strategy, but I don't care. If Piero gets Aida to safety, that's all that matters.

27

AIDA

My heart skips a beat as I watch Malachy and Milo exchange jabs.

It's impossible not to worry, as Milo has taken a lot of bad hits. Malachy looks like a natural-born fighter—as though he has been doing it all his life.

Milo manages to land a fist on his jaw.

Malachy hardly bats an eyelid, bring his fist hard into his stomach.

The grunt of pain from Milo makes me panic.

Why the hell did he come in here alone?

I feel powerlessness as all I can do is watch as Milo gets beaten up by this madman. How is it that I went from hating Milo for his cruel, vindictive ways to loving him so much it hurts? Loving him so much that I knew staying in Boston would be too painful as he constantly turned me away and shut me out.

A movement to my right catches my eye, and I

notice Piero sneaking toward me. I smile at the sight of him. It looks like Milo does have a plan after all.

Weirdly, we've encountered each other many times, but Milo has never taken the time to introduce me to him properly. I only know his name because I heard Milo address him.

He's slow and careful as he moves, making sure Malachy doesn't notice him. I watch him as he pulls out a knife and cuts the bindings that hold me to the chair. Piero shrugs off his jacket and passes it to me.

I hug it around myself, only then realizing I'm sitting here with my breasts out. I give Piero a nod in thanks and take his outstretched hand.

Milo is still fighting with Malachy, and he's not doing too well. His nose is busted up, and his face is bleeding. All I want to do is to run to him, but I know I can't. I can't even ask Piero what the plan is to get him out without risking being heard.

He nods toward the wall, and we both walk toward it carefully and quietly.

"Where the fuck do you two think you are going?" Malachy shouts, his back still turned to us.

Does this guy have eyes in the back of his head?

Piero grabs me and pushes me behind him, blocking me with his body.

Malachy turns to face us. "I don't know if you take me for a fool, but your pathetic attempt to fight me, Milo, was a distraction."

Milo is on the floor, looking pained as he tries to get up.

Malachy reaches for something around his waist, drawing Milo's gun. My heart rate accelerates as he points it at us.

Piero tenses. "Stay behind me, signora." He places his arms behind himself, blocking me in.

Milo speaks, "Malachy, don't you fucking—"

Malachy shoves his boot against Milo's throat, shutting him up. It's hard to see a man so strong and powerful reduced to that position, fighting to get out from under his weight.

"Don't what, Milo?" He glares down at him. "Don't shoot your right-hand man and whore of a wife?" He shakes his head. "I don't like being told what to do."

Malachy releases Milo and walks toward us, keeping the gun trained on Piero.

I watch as Milo struggles to get up from the floor and stand. Our eyes meet for a moment, and I feel an odd sense of calm at the look of determination in his eyes.

Until the gunshot pierces the silence, and Piero crumples to the floor in front of me. Malachy laughs like he's enjoying this too much. Piero is clutching his stomach on the floor as blood pools beneath him, making me feel uneasy.

Thankfully, Milo tackles Malachy to the ground, knocking the gun a few meters away. "You'll pay for shooting my capo, Malachy." He punches him hard in the face, pummeling him with punch after punch. All the while, Malachy delights in the pain and punishment before pushing Milo off him.

Milo is closer to me, and the longing to go run into his protective arms is clawing at me, but I can't seem to get my legs to move. I'm frozen in fear.

"Pathetic attempt, Milo," he says, spitting blood onto the floor as if he's used to taking beatings like that daily. Out of nowhere, he draws another gun and aims it right at him.

Milo holds his hands up. "You don't want to kill me, Malachy." He shakes his head. "You know how much heat you would face if you did. The mayor is about to put me on the city council. It's not like I'm some street rat you can bury in a ditch."

"No, you're right. I won't kill you." Malachy looks frantic as he aims the gun at me instead, making my heart rate accelerate. "You took something precious from me, you bastard. So, I'll take something precious from you." He cocks the gun, and I'm sure I'm about to die.

Milo starts toward me. I can see him running almost in slow motion as Malachy's finger presses down on the trigger without hesitation. The bullet travels through the air toward me.

I want to will my limbs to move, but I'm a deer caught in the headlights, waiting to be hit.

Milo's body connects with mine suddenly as the sound of a bullet hitting flesh fills the air.

I don't feel any pain, other than the ache of being knocked over by a man double my size.

"Milo?" I reach for him and find him covered in blood. "Fuck."

Shots go off somewhere else in the warehouse, and Malachy swears. "Don't any of you fucking move," he growls, heading toward the commotion.

I shift from underneath Milo and cradle his head. "You've been shot." I feel tears welling in my eyes at the fact that he would throw himself in front of a bullet to save my life. I tear a piece off his shirt and hold it against the wound in his shoulder, trying to stem the flow of blood.

Milo tries to move, but I hold him still.

"Don't move." It breaks me to see him in pain, even after all the heartache he's put me through. "You're going to make it worse."

He grunts. "I'm fine." His reaction is short and sharp, the opposite to my reaction about being reunited with him. "It's a flesh wound."

"How do you know?" I ask, narrowing my eyes at him.

He glares right back. "Trust me, princess. I've been shot enough times to know."

A guy I've never seen runs over to us, and I tense, wondering if it's one of Malachy's men. "Boss, we need to get out of here. The other three are providing a distraction."

Milo tries to get to his feet by himself, but I have to help him. The other guy helps Piero to his feet.

"Come on. There's an exit at the back."

I shoulder as much of Milo's weight as I can, but he's heavy. "You have to help me," I say.

Milo grunts in response. "You shouldn't have fucking run, and we wouldn't be in this situation."

Pain clutches around my throat as I wonder if his gallant act was nothing more than just that: an act.

Why did he come for me if he doesn't care?

"I wouldn't have run if you weren't such a dick."

He grunts. "Well, I saved your life. I wouldn't call that being a dick."

Guilt coils through me. I shouldn't be calling him a dick after he threw himself in front of a bullet for me. I keep quiet as we step out of the back exit where an SUV is parked with the engine running. I'm relieved when I see James in the driver's seat.

I help Milo into the back, and the other guy gets Piero into the passenger's seat.

"How the fuck are Angelo, Pietro, and Ramon getting out of there?" James asks.

The other guy replies, "Drive around the front. You've got to pick them up inside."

"Inside?" I ask.

The guy turns around and smirks at me. "Yeah, we're going in. So hold on tight, signora."

As James pulls around the warehouse building, my

brow furrows. James puts his foot down, racing toward the front of the building.

I fumble to put my belt in, noticing that Milo isn't belted in either. The SUV crashes through the warehouse's front as bullets ricochet off the armored body of the vehicle.

Three guys get into the SUV with machine guns, while the guy who rescued us covers them from the shots of Malachy and his men.

I swallow hard as he notices me and aims the gun at me, narrowing his eyes as he tries to focus on shooting me from a distance.

I duck out of fear that he would get through the armored shell of the SUV.

James slams into reverse fast, doing a u-turn to drive forward and away from the warehouse. Bullets rebound off the outer shell of the vehicle as James drives us away.

Milo groans as we drive over the bumpy terrain out of the docks.

I grab hold of his hand and squeeze. "Are you okay?" I murmur.

He grits his teeth. "Not exactly. I've been shot." I try to pull my hand from his, but he grabs it back. "Sorry. I'm pissed off that Malachy bested me."

I shake my head. "Does it matter? We're both alive and safe."

Milo glares at me. "You don't understand what this means." He groans and bites his lip. "I hate the fucking

Irish." He tightens his grip on my hand and looks me in the eye. "Why did you run?"

I shrug, despite knowing exactly why I ran.

"Tell me, Aida."

I meet his gaze, and the fear of rejection almost cripples me. "I couldn't stay while you continue to break my heart over and over again."

Milo's gaze softens, and he brings the back of my hand to his lips, kissing gently. "I'm sorry." His throat bobs, and he looks at me with a mournful expression. "If you want to return to Sicily, then I'll allow it."

I can hardly believe what he's saying. "What?"

"I will release you from our marriage and let you go home if that's what you want."

I stare at him, trying to work out if that's what I want. It's not. All I want is for this man to love me the way I love him.

I bite the inside of my cheek, wondering if he will break my heart again if I open up to him. Every time things have gotten serious; he has pulled away. "It hurts so much, Milo." I shake my head. "I know you made it clear to me what this was between us from the start, but…"

"But what, angel?"

I glance through to the next row of seats, making sure his men aren't listening. Piero is sitting in front of us, groaning in pain as one of the guys helps him stem the blood flowing from his wound. I hope he pulls through, as it has become clear to me that Piero is the closest thing Milo has to a friend. He trusts him more than his other men. The others are talking about the crazy rescue mission they pulled off.

"I love you. It's crazy and makes no sense, but it's the truth." I move closer to him and kiss his lips softly, savoring the feel of his skin on mine. "I don't want to be without you," I murmur.

He smiles at me and kisses the back of my hand again. "I'm glad to hear it. I want you to stay."

I swallow hard, knowing that although it's not the dreaded rejection I feared, it isn't exactly what I wanted to hear.

All I can think is, *does he love me too?*

He coughs suddenly, and I notice he's looking paler than before. It's not the time to be having this conversation. Milo has lost too much blood, and he needs to see a doctor.

"Relax, Milo. We'll get you help soon," I say, squeezing his hand.

The least of my worries is whether he loves me or not. Milo has been shot, and even if he's sure it's a flesh wound, he might not make it through. That's a thought that scares me more than anything.

28

MILO

The rhythmic beeping of the heart monitor set up in my room is the first thing I register when I wake. The second is Aida lying by my side, fast asleep. It still angers me when I see the cuts that are starting to heal on her perfect skin, some of which will leave scars.

Thankfully, they were superficial. I feel guilty because when Aida arrived in Boston, she was untainted. Her scars will be a permanent reminder that pushing her away landed her in the hands of my enemy.

War has broken out. Malachy hit back at one of my venues in the city, blowing it up and making it look like a gas leak. Angelo is handling our counterattack, but we have a long and rocky road ahead of us.

Piero is doing okay, but his gunshot wound was worse than mine. He'll be out of action for a while.

After him, Angelo is the only man I could trust within my operation to run things. Casualties are inevitable in a war, and I need to start getting to know which guys I can trust if any of my lieutenants meet their demise in this war.

I return my attention to Aida, who won't leave my side ever since I was shot by Malachy four days ago. It makes no sense why she cares so much. After the way I've treated her since we met, she should hate me.

I told her I'd let her go back to Sicily if she preferred, and I was surprised but relieved when she declined. Instead, she professed her love for me, telling me she never wants to leave my side. My response probably wasn't what she wanted, but I told her I'd like her to stay.

I know I need to tell her the truth. I need to tell her that when Malachy took her, I hadn't been that scared since my mother was in the hospital.

Aida stirs, opening her eyes. She looks adorable when she's sleepy. Aida smiles lazily at me when she sees that I'm awake. A smile I can't get enough of seeing. "Hi," she says, rubbing a hand across her face and yawning.

"Hey, princess."

She stretches and sits up in our bed. "How are you feeling?"

I smile. "Almost back to normal."

She shakes her head. "That's not what the doctor said. He's prescribed at least another four days in bed."

I groan. "It's too fucking boring lying in bed doing nothing." I glance at my wife and place a hand on her thighs. "How about you make it more exciting for me?"

Aida shifts out of my grasp. "No. The doctor's order is to rest. Nothing strenuous."

I clench my jaw, hating being told what to do. "You know I hate being told no, angel."

Aida jumps off the bed, shrugging. "It's not like I said no. It was the doctor."

I raise a brow. "The doctor's not here now." I pat the empty side of the bed again. "Come here," I order.

She obeys me and sits by my side.

I take her hand in mine, knowing it's now or never. There's no use putting this off. I might as well rip off the band-aid. "I'm sorry for pulling away from you constantly."

The column of her throat gently bobs as she swallows. "I can't say you didn't warn me what our relationship would be like." She laughs nervously.

I shake my head. "Well, I was wrong, princess. Something I hardly ever admit to." I lift a hand to her cheek and cup it gently. "When I found out that you were gone, I haven't felt that scared since..." I swallow hard, feeling my defenses fight against the need to tell her the truth, "my mother."

Aida's eyes brim with tears as she listens to me. "Milo—"

I hold a hand up to silence her. "Let me finish, mio amore."

Her eyes widen when she hears me call her "my love" in Italian, and the tears start to rush down her perfect skin.

"When I found out that Malachy took you, it was the most terrifying moment of my life." I shake my head. "The fear of losing you." I squeeze her hand and bring it up to my lips, kissing the back of it. "What I'm trying to say, quite badly, is, I-I love you with all of my heart." I let out a shaky breath. The last time I spoke those three words, I was seven years old, and my mother was dying in a hospital bed.

Aida's tears flood down her cheeks as she smiles at me, shaking her head. "I hope this isn't a cruel joke you're playing on me."

A growl rises in my chest at the idea that she could think I would hurt her that badly. "Never, angel. I may have been cruel to you when we first met, but even I'm not that sick." I grab hold of her and pull her to me, kissing her passionately.

I allow the emotion I've feared for most of my life to flood me: love.

It's unexpected. When I agreed to marry Fabio's daughter, I never could have imagined I'd feel this way about her. She challenges me and excites me. She makes me a better man, and for that, I'll be eternally grateful.

It helps that she doesn't take my shit lying down. She fights me every step of the way, and I admire her for it.

When we break apart, we're both panting for breath. "I need to be inside of you," I murmur against Aida's lips.

She sets her hands on my shoulders and meets my gaze with a desire that sets my body on fire. "I want to, but the doctor told you to rest."

I smirk. "How about you do the work, and I rest?" I throw the duvet off myself, pull the heart monitor pads off my chest, and pull down my boxer briefs, revealing my cock hard and ready to take her. "Come and ride me, angel."

She licks her lips before nodding eagerly.

I watch her as she pulls off her nightdress. Aida positions herself over me, holding my gaze. She loves being in this position of power over me, but I know it won't last long once she starts. My need to dominate will rule over the doctor's order to rest.

"That's it, mio amore, sit on daddy's dick."

She moans as she sits down on my cock, sheathing me in her tight, wet cunt.

I groan as my balls ache for release almost instantly. It's been too long since I was inside my angel. This is where I belong.

Aida moves her hips up and down as she grinds on my cock, moaning with each movement she makes.

I wrap an arm around her back and lean forward to suck on her hard nipples. Aida moans a high-pitched and sensual sound that drives me wild.

"Don't get used to being on top, though," I say,

gently teasing my teeth around her hard nipples and making her pussy gush over my cock.

"Fuck, daddy," she moans, eyes clamped shut as she rides me harder and faster.

I grab hold of her hips and take control of her. "I want to look into your eyes as you ride me."

Aida's eyes open, and she meets my gaze.

I drive her hips up and down at my speed, taking control while she's on top of me.

"You are supposed to be resting, daddy," she whines, trying to pull my hands off her hips.

"No, angel, I'm supposed to be fucking my naughty little wife." I wrap an arm around her waist and lift her effortlessly, forcing her down onto her back.

She gasps. "Milo, what about your wound?"

I grunt. There's a dull ache, but nothing more. "I'm fine, mio amore. Now keep quiet and take my cock like a good girl."

Aida squeals in delight as I pound into her so hard the bed starts to rock. Her pussy muscles clamp down on me tightly as I drive toward the edge, hitting that magic spot inside of her that makes her come. "Yes, daddy, fuck me harder," she cries, eyes shut again.

I spank her thigh. "Eyes open. I want to look into them as you come all over my cock like my dirty little whore."

Aida bites her lip and opens her eyes.

I stare into them as I thrust my hips harder and faster, feeling such an intimate connection with the woman beneath me. I never expected to get married, and I certainly didn't expect to fall in love with her.

As we both near our mutual climaxes, I feel that desperate, primal need to her breed her wash over me again. It's crazy since I can't even imagine being a father. Yet, every time I'm inside of my angel, it feels like it's the sole reason I'm on this earth. It gives me a purpose that I can't fully comprehend.

I growl against the skin at her neck, kissing a path to her jaw. I bite her earlobe, making her whine. When I return to look her in the eyes, they're entirely dilated with a need that matches my own. "I need to breed you. I want you growing big and round with my baby."

Aida bites her bottom lip. "Yes, daddy, breed me. I want all of your cum deep inside of me."

I growl again, feeling an unparalleled need taking hold of me. At that moment, all my worries melt away. It's as if the only thing that matters anymore is the woman beneath me. As if we are the only two people that exist in this world. I wish it were the truth.

"Oh fuck, daddy, I'm going to come," she whines, driving me wild with need as I pound into her even harder.

It's hard to believe she was a virgin when we married. Aida is the first woman I've ever met who loves fucking as rough as I do. "That's it, mio amore. Look in daddy's eyes while you come on my cock."

She cries out, holding my gaze as she tumbles over the edge of the cliff. Her muscles tighten around my shaft, forcing me to climax right along with her. "Fuck," I growl, pumping into her repeatedly as I unleash every drop of seed deep inside of her.

Aida squeals in surprise when I grab her hips and flip her onto all fours. "There's something I have to do, princess." I bury my tongue into her tight asshole, and she tries to pull away in surprise.

Ever since I took her virginity, I've wanted to fuck her virgin ass too. I pull her hips closer to me to stop her from escaping. "Don't move, angel."

She groans. "What are you–"

I spank her ass before she can question me. "No questions, unless you want me to punish you." I grab hold of a pair of handcuffs off the nightstand and clamp them around her wrists, making sure she can't escape.

She stills as I continue to lick her, making her pussy drip even more.

"I know you love having your ass licked because you're my dirty little whore, aren't you?"

Aida moans, nodding her head.

I spank her ass cheek. "I want to hear you tell me how much you like it."

Aida tenses as I return my tongue to her hole. "I love it, daddy," she whines, but there's a tension in her voice.

A sudden thought occurs to me that she may not like it at all. "Aida, you can tell me if you want me to stop," I say.

She shakes her head. "No, I don't. It's just…"

"What is it?" I ask, feeling impatient as my cock throbs between my thighs.

"Are you going to fuck me there?"

I want that more than anything. "Do you want me to?" It feels weird asking for permission, but I know that she should have the right to decide.

"I think so, but I'm scared it will hurt."

I shake my head. "Don't worry about that. I'll make sure it's painless."

She relaxes slightly. "Okay, I trust you," she says in a sultry voice that has me leaking precum all over the bedsheets.

I reach for a bottle of lube in the nightstand and squirt a generous amount on her tight little hole.

She squeals in surprise. "That's cold, daddy."

Fuck. This girl is going to be the death of me. I need to be in her tight little ass, but I know I have no choice but to take this slow.

"Yes, angel, but it's going to feel good soon."

I slide a finger into her tight passage, groaning at the way her muscles clench it like a vice. My cock jumps at the mere thought of being inside her.

Slowly, I stretch her hole, first one finger, then two, then three. By the time I'm on to the fourth, she's begging me to keep going. Once her hole is loose enough to take my four fingers fucking her easily, I decide it's time to try my cock.

Aida is panting and moaning as I slide my fingers out. She whimpers in protest. "Don't stop, daddy."

I smirk at her eagerness. "Don't worry, angel, I'm not stopping. It's time to try my cock."

She moans as I fist my heavy, throbbing dick in my hands. I've never been so turned on in my entire life.

Slowly, I drag the tip of my cock over her gaping hole. "Are you ready for me to fuck your ass, angel?"

She nods. "Yes, I'm so ready."

"Good girl," I say before adding more lube to her hole and my cock to ensure I don't hurt her. It's a new sensation for me, caring whether I hurt someone.

I push against her hole and slide the head of my cock through her tight ring of muscles.

Aida groans. "Fuck, that hurts," she says.

I run a hand over the curve of her spine. "Relax and breathe. It'll only hurt for a short while. Give it time."

My voice calms her as she relaxes, and slowly my cock slides deeper inside. It's tighter than I ever could have imagined. My cock leaks deep in her ass, making me groan.

"Fuck, your ass feels like heaven wrapped around my cock," I growl.

"Fuck my ass, daddy," she moans.

I pull my cock slowly out of her tight hole, watching as her tight muscles try to pull me back inside.

The need to breed every one of her holes takes

control of me. Aida has a way of turning me into a beast.

I thrust back into her hard, and she cries out in a sound that embodies a mix of pain and pleasure. A sound that only spurs on the deep, dark need to master her body in every way.

Her tight, virgin hole resists me at first. The size of my cock stretches her more than my fingers did.

"Fuck," she cries as I lose control, pounding into her with uncontrolled thrusts.

"That's it, angel. Take daddy's cock in that tight ass," I growl.

She arches her back, allowing me to sink deeper. "Yes, daddy."

My obedient wife is a marvel to me. The way we both fit together like two missing pieces of a whole is astounding. It's as though fate brought us together.

"Fuck," I grunt as I feel my balls clench. "I need you to come for me." I rub her clit, which makes her moan.

I feel her muscles tightening around me as I continue to pound into her. It makes me feel powerful, knowing I've claimed all her holes first. She belongs to me and no one else.

"Fuck, yes," she cries out as she tumbles over the edge. Her muscles are so tight as she climaxes.

I come at the same time, filling her virgin hole with my seed. It drives me crazy to think she will have my cum dripping out of both holes all day. We're both panting for breath as I stop moving inside of her. Slowly, I pull my cock out of her ass and sit back on my haunches.

I take in the sight of her pussy and ass dripping with my cum. It is the best sight I've ever seen in my life. "Lie down," I say.

She collapses on the bed, lying on her back with her wrist pressed against her forehead. "That was insane…"

"Insanely good, I hope?"

She smiles at me and nods.

I lie down by her side and pull her against me. Initially, she tenses, looking up at me quizzically, as if she never expected me to hold her after we fucked.

"I'm not sure how you can forgive me for all the bullshit I've put you through."

She sighs. "I guess that's what happens when you love someone. You take a lot of shit from them." She smiles up at me. "Luckily, you decided to stop being an ass before I ran away."

I shake my head and give her ass a gentle spank. "Don't speak to me like that unless you want to be punished."

Suddenly, her eyes widen. "Fuck, I forgot about your gunshot wound that entire time."

I laugh. "Don't worry about it, angel. I'm almost healed. It was only a flesh wound, and the doctor is cautious." I shrug. "Plus, the painkillers help."

She rests her head on my chest, burying her face

against my skin. "I'm so glad you are okay. I don't know what I'd do if I lost you."

A sentiment I find hard to believe. How could a man as cold as me be lucky enough to have found a woman who managed to find a way to love me?

I'll never know the answer. All my life, I've been a zombie walking through the world without feeling anything. It took a feisty woman to fight me every step of the way and challenge me in ways I never knew possible to open my eyes up to what I've been missing. I'll cherish her forever.

"I can't wait to spend the rest of my life with you, angel," I murmur, stroking my hand through her dark, soft hair. We fall silent together, wrapped in the blissful glow of our love.

EPILOGUE

AIDA

One year later...

I sit on my favorite beach outside of Palermo with my toes in the surf. Milo swims a few meters from the shore, confidently stroking through the waves.

It took a while for me to convince him to visit my favorite place in the world, especially since the war we've been embroiled in with the Irish is far from over. Milo also landed a seat on the city council three months after he rescued me from Malachy. It gives him more power in his fight against Malachy, and he's used that power to attack his operations legally.

Both Malachy and Milo are too proud to agree on a truce as they can't find common ground. However, there have been signs that Malachy might want to lay the weapons down ever since Milo managed to block half his shipments coming into port.

Life in Boston is more challenging than I could have imagined since he's been having issues with the Russians too. It has been one hell of a challenging first year of marriage, but it has made me stronger.

Milo finally agreed to come to Sicily because my father has offered him support in the war. I haven't seen my best friends in a year, as he insisted it was too dangerous for them to visit Boston while the war rages on.

He met my father an hour after we arrived out of courtesy, but I didn't want to see him. After what he did to me, I never want to see him again. I was surprised when Milo tried to convince me to rethink not seeing him since our first child is on his or her way.

My father will be our child's only living grandparent. Maybe I shouldn't be so angry at him since he thrust me into the arms of a monster who I fell head over heels in love with, even if the journey to happiness with Milo was anything but easy sailing. For all my father knew, he could have been sending me off to an early demise, and he didn't care.

Milo finishes his swim and stands in the ocean, shaking his hair out and running his hands through it.

My stomach does a flip at the sight of the water cascading down his chiseled, tattooed body as the sun hits him in a way that makes him look angelic. I smile to myself. Milo is so far from angelic, but I've grown to love that dark side of him.

"What are you smiling at, angel?"

I shrug. "How lucky I am to be married to a fucking god," I say, knowing how much he loves me flattering him.

"God, hey?" Milo sits behind me with his legs on either side of me and his arms around my waist. "How are you enjoying being home?"

I contemplate his question, wondering if I can call this home now. The home I grew up in is off-limits since I don't want to see my father.

It feels more like a holiday than a visit to my home. "Sicily is no longer my home."

Milo presses his lips to my shoulder. "No?"

I shake my head. "You are," I reply.

He chuckles softly behind me. "That's cheesy."

I sigh heavily. "It's how I feel. Boston has become my home because of you, Milo."

He nibbles on the lobe of my ear. "Shut up, princess." He bites my shoulder.

"Aida, oh my God!" Gia shouts my name and screams, running toward us.

Milo groans. "I'm so glad we don't live near your friends, and I haven't even met them yet."

I elbow him in the stomach. "Don't be an ass."

I stand up from the beach and greet my friend, who wraps me in a tight hug. "It's been too long since I last saw you," I say, feeling the tears spilling down my cheeks at the relief of seeing my best friend again after an entire year away from Sicily.

Siena is trailing behind, smiling as she approaches.

"We have both missed you," she says, patting my shoulder.

I release myself from Gia's embrace and hug Siena. "Boston is a shit hole compared to here," I say.

They both laugh, stopping suddenly and glancing behind me. Milo places a hand on my shoulder and squeezes hard. "Aren't you going to introduce me?"

I roll my eyes, knowing he can't see me from behind.

Gia and Siena don't laugh. They both look a little shaken by my giant of a husband. I guess he's a little intimidating, but I've gotten used to it by now. "Gia and Siena, this is my husband, Milo." I turn to look at him. "Milo, this is Gia and Siena, my two best friends."

"It's lovely to meet you," Gia and Siena say in unison.

Milo nods. "Good to meet you too." He glances at me. "I'll let you three catch up." He places his hands on either side of my waist and leans down to my ear. "Don't be too long, angel. I don't like waiting." He kisses my neck before turning away and walking back toward the sea.

"At least your arranged marriage landed you with a hot husband," Siena says.

I laugh, since it's true, but if they knew all I'd been through with Milo, they may not be so enamored by his good looks.

Gia grabs my hand and looks me in the eye. "Aren't you intending to see your father while you are here?"

I shake my head. "No chance in hell. After what he did to me, I'm not sure I'll ever want to see him again."

Gia looks disappointed by my answer, and I can't understand why. "I think he regrets what he did to you, Aida."

My brow furrows, and I remember our conversation when she said she would visit him. "Don't tell me you ignored me and went to speak to him?"

Gia shrugs. "I'm sorry. I couldn't sit by while he ripped my best friend away from me like that." There's a look of guilt in her eyes.

"Did he say he wished he hadn't done it?"

Gia doesn't look me in the eye, which is weird. She's never normally like this. "He admitted what he did and how he went about it was wrong."

I shake my head. "If that's the case, I'd expect him to track me down and apologize. There's no way I'm running to him."

Siena nods. "Yeah, what he did was not okay."

Gia nods but doesn't say anymore.

"I don't want to spoil my time here thinking about him." I glance at my husband, who's returned to swim in the sea. "Will both of you join us for dinner tonight?" I ask.

Siena and Gia exchange glances, looking a little uncertain. "We're supposed to attend your father's annual ball tonight. Isn't Milo invited?"

I clench my jaw. "Yes, but Milo isn't attending out of respect for me." The fact that my best friends would rather attend the ball than have dinner with me is irritating, but I know how this island works.

The annual ball is the hottest social event of the year, and everyone who is anyone attends. It makes me realize how small my world was when I lived here in Sicily.

"Never mind. We can have dinner tomorrow night," I say.

Gia looks relieved, but Siena looks a little disappointed. "I can't believe we have to wait an entire day until we can catch up," she says.

I glance at my watch, noticing that it's almost four o'clock in the afternoon. "You better get ready, or you'll be late for the ball. If you feel up to it, you can spend the day with us tomorrow as we've hired a yacht."

Siena nods enthusiastically. "That sounds amazing, doesn't it, Gia?"

She shrugs. "I'm not sure I'll be able to make it tomorrow. I'll try." Her phone rings and she answers it, walking away.

"Gia seems a little…"

"Distracted?" Siena offers.

I nod in response.

"Yes, she's been like that for a while. Ever since she met some guy that she won't tell me anything about."

I raise a brow. "Is that who she is talking to?"

"God knows. She's been so private. So, I'll see you tomorrow?"

I nod. "Sure. The yacht leaves at ten in the morning from here."

"Sounds great. I'll see you then." She pulls me into a long hug, then turns and rushes after Gia, who didn't even say goodbye. There's something odd going on with her.

I head toward the sea, dropping my beach dress on the sand. Milo stops swimming and comes into the shallows to meet me. "Your friends didn't stay long."

I shake my head, setting my hands on his shoulders. "No, Gia was acting weird. They're going to the ball tonight and can't make dinner."

Milo wraps his arms around my waist. "Are you sure you don't want to go?"

I stare up at him. "I'm sure. I don't want to see him, Milo. We talked about this."

Milo nods. "I know, princess." He shrugs. "You wouldn't have to see him. There'll be hundreds of people at the ball."

I glare at him. "No, I don't want to risk bumping into him." Milo does listen to me more now than when we first met, but if he tried to force me to go to my father's ball, I wouldn't be happy.

He kisses me softly before murmuring against my ear, "Whatever you want, but only because this concerns your family." He nips my bottom lip softly. "Don't get used to it, angel."

I pull back and give him a defiant glare, as he loves it when I fight. "Maybe I should get used to it." I turn away from him and run toward the sea, glancing back over my shoulder at him. "I'm going for a swim."

Milo's growl follows me as I rush toward the warm Mediterranean Sea. "You know I love it when you run."

Excitement twists my stomach because I know he's going to chase me. I love being chased as much as he loves chasing. I make it to the surf. As I'm about to dive into the sea, Milo grabs me around the waist and lifts me off my feet.

"Hey, I didn't even get a chance to dive in."

Milo's deep, gruff voice purrs in my ear, "No swimming for you, but you're going to be very wet when I'm through with you, angel."

My thighs clench as he carries me away from the sea, heading back toward the villa we rented on the beach.

"Let me go. I haven't had my swim," I whine, putting up a fight as I know how much Milo loves my resistance.

It's ironic that when we met, all I wanted was to get away from this man. After just over a year married to him, all I want is to please him. He takes care of me, and I love him for it.

Milo sets me down on a large day bed by our villa pool and stares down at me silently.

"What are you looking at?" I ask.

He smiles. "A work of fucking art. You're perfect. Have I told you that?"

I shrug. "About a hundred times, but no one is perfect."

He kneels in front of me on the daybed and parts my legs so he can get closer to me. "That's not true. You are perfect to me, mio amore." He gently slides my bikini bottoms off before dipping his head to meet my aching pussy.

I cry out as he circles my clit with the tip of his tongue, making me needy. I'm always needy around my husband, but once he touches me, the need takes control.

He doesn't stop there, plunging his tongue deep inside of me and tasting me. I'm wound up tighter than a coiled spring.

It's crazy that my desire for my husband only grows daily. Our relationship has blossomed into something stronger than I could have imagined. The saying that there is a fine line between love and hate most certainly is true, as we're the living proof.

Milo slides two fingers inside of me, curling them to hit the spot that makes me cry out every time. He knows my body better than I do. Slowly, he drives me closer and closer to climax, only to deny me every time.

He has taught me that patience for release makes it ten times more explosive. Even so, it's impossible not to feel frustrated.

"Please, sir, make me come," I beg.

He chuckles. "Not until I'm buried deep inside of you, princess."

"Then fuck me," I say.

He smirks up at me with one eyebrow raised. "Fuck me what?"

I know what he wants me to say. "Fuck me, please, daddy."

"Good girl." He slides his swim shorts down, releasing his huge, hard cock. It bobs back and slaps into his chiseled abs. He lines himself up with me and slides all the way inside with one stroke.

Milo grabs hold of my wrists and pins them above me on the day bed, restraining me. Slowly, he moves his hips in and out. Each stroke is hard but slow, so I can feel every inch of him sinking all the way in before pulling all the way back out. He holds my gaze, grunting like an animal.

"I will never get enough of you, Aida," he growls, leaning down to nibble at the flesh above my collarbone. "Never," he murmurs. He bites me, sending a thrilling pain through my nerve endings and setting them on fire.

"I'll never get enough of you, daddy," I cry as his thrusts get faster. Ever since I fell pregnant, he's become less rough with me and more protective than ever. I love it when he's rough, but he doesn't feel right being too rough or tying me up too much while I'm pregnant.

"Fuck me harder," I beg, trying to break free from his hold on my wrists.

Milo growls softly, "Don't move, princess." He tries to hold himself back. The strained look on his face tells me that much. He lets go of my wrists and places his hand around my throat in a firm grip. "I want you to come for me on command. Do you understand?"

I nod in response, "Yes, daddy."

"Fuck," he roars. "Then come now for me."

He is the master of my body, as his order is all it takes. White-hot pleasure courses through every nerve in my body as my release slams into me. My muscles tighten around his cock as if they never want him to leave. Milo is so deep inside of me I don't know where I end and he begins. It feels like I'm floating and my only anchor to this world is my husband.

Milo releases my throat and bites my shoulder as he comes inside of me, shooting rope after rope of seed.

For a while, we remain in that position in silence, staring into each other's eyes. The intimacy between us only increases the longer we're together. At times, it feels like he can see right into my soul.

Milo collapses next to me on the day bed, pulling me against him. "Aida, you're my addiction," he murmurs, curling his fingers in my hair. "I can't get enough."

I smile and nestle against his warm, muscular body. "Good. I hope you never get enough."

He laughs. "I can't wait to start a family with you." He shakes his head. "Fuck, I never thought I'd say those words to anyone."

I reach up and cup his face. "Neither can I. I love you more than anything."

He looks into my eyes, and I see tears of joy brimming in them. They don't fall, but I can see how much he cares.

It's crazy when I think back to the man that I met over a year ago. Our love story was anything but traditional, but real life isn't like fairytales. In real life, the princess falls in love with the villain more often than not. I'm just lucky that my villain loves me back.

Thank you for reading Cruel Daddy, the first book in my Boston Mafia Doms series. I hope you enjoyed following Milo and Aida's story.

The next book in this series follows Irish mobster Malachy McCarthy's twisted romance story. This book is available through Kindle Unlimited or to buy on Amazon.

Savage Daddy: A Dark Captive Mafia Romance

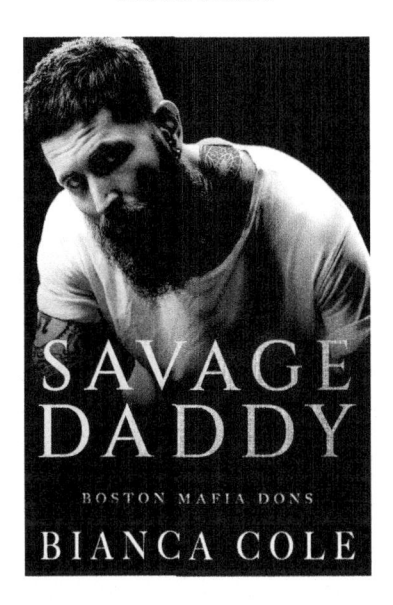

Desperation led me into the hands of a savage.

I should never have considered auctioning my virginity. The kind of men likely to bid are the type you never want to meet. Dark, twisted, and dangerous.

Malachy is no exception. He buys me at the auction. He takes me home and locks me away.

It turns out selling your virginity has an entirely different meaning to what I thought. I expect one night, and then I'm free. Not when it comes to Malachy McCarthy.

I belong to him until he says so. A toy to play with until he decides he's bored. The man is a savage, and I'm his next meal.

I don't know if I'll come out at the end of this in

one piece. More importantly, I'm not sure I can keep my heart untouched. Will this savage bend and break that as well?

Savage Daddy is the second book in the Boston Mafia Doms Series by Bianca Cole. This book is a safe story with no cliffhangers and a happily ever after ending. This story has dark themes that may upset some people, hot scenes, and bad language. It features an over-the-top, twisted, and savage Irish mobster.

ALSO BY BIANCA COLE

The Syndicate Academy

Corrupt Educator: A Dark Forbidden Mafia Academy Romance

Cruel Bully: A Dark Mafia Academy Romance

Chicago Mafia Dons

Merciless Defender: A Dark Forbidden Mafia Romance

Violent Leader: A Dark Enemies to Lovers Captive Mafia Romance

Evil Prince: A Dark Arranged Marriage Romance

Brutal Daddy: A Dark Captive Mafia Romance

Cruel Vows: A Dark Forced Marriage Mafia Romance

Dirty Secret: A Dark Enemies to Loves Mafia Romance

Dark Crown: A Dark Arranged Marriage Romance

Boston Mafia Dons Series

Cruel Daddy: A Dark Mafia Arranged Marriage Romance

Savage Daddy: A Dark Captive Mafia Roamnce

Ruthless Daddy: A Dark Forbidden Mafia Romance

Vicious Daddy: A Dark Brother's Best Friend Mafia Romance

Wicked Daddy: A Dark Captive Mafia Romance

New York Mafia Doms Series

Her Irish Daddy: A Dark Mafia Romance

Her Russian Daddy: A Dark Mafia Romance

Her Italian Daddy: A Dark Mafia Romance

Her Cartel Daddy: A Dark Mafia Romance

Romano Mafia Brother's Series

Her Mafia Daddy: A Dark Daddy Romance

Her Mafia Boss: A Dark Romance

Her Mafia King: A Dark Romance

Bratva Brotherhood Series

Bought by the Bratva: A Dark Mafia Romance

Captured by the Bratva: A Dark Mafia Romance

Claimed by the Bratva: A Dark Mafia Romance

Bound by the Bratva: A Dark Mafia Romance

Taken by the Bratva: A Dark Mafia Romance

Wynton Series

Filthy Boss: A Forbidden Office Romance

Filthy Professor: A First Time Professor And Student Romance

Filthy Lawyer: A Forbidden Hate to Love Romance

Filthy Doctor: A Fordbidden Romance

Royally Mated Series

Her Faerie King: A Faerie Royalty Paranormal Romance

Her Alpha King: A Royal Wolf Shifter Paranormal Romance

Her Dragon King: A Dragon Shifter Paranormal Romance

Her Vampire King: A Dark Vampire Romance

ABOUT THE AUTHOR

I love to write stories about over the top alpha bad boys who have heart beneath it all, fiery heroines, and happily-ever-after endings with heart and heat. My stories have twists and turns that will keep you flipping the pages and heat to set your kindle on fire.

For as long as I can remember, I've been a sucker for a good romance story. I've always loved to read. Suddenly, I realized why not combine my love of two things, books and romance?

My love of writing has grown over the past four years and I now publish on Amazon exclusively, weaving stories about dirty mafia bad boys and the women they fall head over heels in love with.

If you enjoyed this book please follow me on Amazon, Bookbub or any of the below social media platforms for alerts when more books are released.